Gr.4.3
6

8-01

BROTHERS IN VALOR

A Story of Resistance

Michael O. Tunnell

Holiday House / New York

For the real Helmuth,
Karl-Heinz, Rudi,
and Gerhard

Quotations on pages 41, 97, 101–102, 105, 106, 107, 111, 130–131, 140, 141–142, 242–243, 248–250 from *When Truth Was Treason: German Youth Against Hitler.* Copyright 1995 by the Board of Trustees of the University of Illinois. Used with the permission of the University of Illinois Press.

Library of Congress Cataloging-in-Publication Data
Tunnell, Michael O.
Brothers in valor : a story of resistance / Michael O. Tunnell.—1st ed.
p. cm.
Summary: Three German teenagers who are members of the Mormon church join forces to create a youth resistance movement during World War II, putting their lives at risk.
ISBN 0-8234-1541-4 (hardcover)
1. World War, 1939–1945—Germany—Juvenile fiction.
[1. World War, 1939–1945—Germany—Fiction. 2. Germany—History—1933–1945 —Fiction. 3. Mormons—Germany—Fiction.] I. Title.
PZ7.T825 Br 2001
[Fic]—dc21   00-054053

National Socialism and
Christianity are irreconcilable.
—MARTIN BORMANN,
DEPUTY LEADER
OF THE NAZI PARTY, 1941

And ye shall know the truth,
and the truth shall make you free.
—JOHN 8:32

Part One

Hamburg,

1937–1939

Chapter One

"You're crazy," said Helmuth. "Certifiable."

"Because I like westerns better than mysteries?" Karl laughed so loud, President Zander peered at us from his office.

"That's right." Helmuth looked at me. "Isn't it, Rudi?"

"Don't drag *me* into this," I said.

Helmuth sighed. "Come on, Rudi, take a stand."

I shrugged. "I like them both."

"No you don't. All you read are mysteries. You just finished another Agatha Christie."

"But he's moving on to Karl May next," Karl said.

"Karl May!" Helmuth laughed. "He has the

nerve to write about cowboys and Indians, but he's never even been to America."

"Has Agatha Christie ever solved a crime?" asked Karl.

"At least Christie *visits* the places she writes about. She talks to police detectives. Karl May wouldn't know a cattle drive if he were caught in a stampede."

President Zander stood next to us now. "But Karl May was German, not British."

"That has nothing to do with it, President Zander," said Helmuth. "It's about being a good writer or not."

"I'd love to discuss this with you, Helmuth, but I'm here to remind you that this is Sunday School. Get to class."

"Please don't tell me *you* like Karl May," Helmuth said. "Please—"

"Stop!" President Zander smiled, pointing in the direction of our classroom.

Arthur Zander was our church leader—the president of our "branch"—but that didn't keep Helmuth from teasing him. This time he kept quiet and grinned at him as we started down the hall.

Helmuth, Karl, and I had been friends since we'd met in our church's program for young children. We were all Mormons—members of The Church of Jesus Christ of Latter-day Saints. Because there weren't many Mormons in Hamburg, church members tried to see one another as much as possible. I'd see Helmuth and Karl on Sundays, in the morning for Sunday School and in the evening for sacrament meeting. Next year, when I turned twelve, I'd be seeing them more often. Helmuth and Karl were both old enough to attend Mutual Improvement Association—MIA—the church's Wednesday evening activities for teenagers. But our friendship wasn't confined to church gatherings. We got together whenever we could, even though we went to different schools in different parts of town.

Before we reached our classroom, President Zander stopped us. "You're good boys," he said, looking straight at Helmuth. "Listen to me. Read *German* books. Listen to *German* music. Play *German* games."

"But our church is American," Helmuth said.

"It's God's church, Helmuth, not America's. Our church leaders want us to be good citizens wherever we live. That means doing what our Führer asks, and he's asked us to be German through and through."

"Don't you mean Nazi through and through?" an ancient voice rattled. It was our Sunday School teacher, Brother Worbs, who had come up behind us. "German and Nazi are not the same thing."

"Is that what you mean, President Zander?" Helmuth's look dared him to answer.

President Zander stared back. "Yes," he finally said. "That's why I joined the Party."

Brother Worbs interrupted. "I missed my star pupils, so I came looking. Let's go, boys."

As we followed him, Helmuth said, "Trust me, Karl. Agatha Christie writes better mysteries than any German. And Zane Grey's westerns are better than May's, even if he *is* an American."

"Well, I *do* like the Lord Lister detective stories," Karl said. "And they're English."

The look on President Zander's face convinced me to keep quiet.

After Sunday School, I found my mother talking to President Zander. I worried that I might be in trouble, but he and Mutti were smiling.

"Rudi, President Zander has a job for you and your friends," Mutti said.

Zander waved Karl and Helmuth over. "Sister Zander and I put together food boxes for the widows in our branch. Would you deliver some of them for me?"

"Just to the sisters who live between here and our place," Mutti added. "Then Helmuth and Karl can join us for lunch, Rudi."

"Sure," said Helmuth, without even checking to see if Karl or I agreed.

"Thank you!" President Zander said. "You'll be blessed for this."

Mutti turned to us. "President and Sister Zander paid for a good part of this themselves."

He blushed a little. "Come along," he said. "I'll get you started."

We followed him to the church kitchen. The food boxes were neatly packed and stacked on the counters. We had a lot of widows in the branch because of the Great War, but the number of boxes still surprised me. There were a dozen for us.

"How will we carry them?" Karl asked, but as always Helmuth was already ahead of us, loading boxes onto a nearby wagon.

"Rudi, you're in charge of the list." President Zander handed me a sheet of paper.

Our church building was a renovated section of an old factory with tall double doors that opened onto a loading dock. We eased the wagon down a ramp and turned to wave to President Zander. He clicked his heels together and started to raise his hand in a Nazi salute, but changed his mind and simply waved back at us.

"Bring back the wagon next time you come."

Helmuth sat down, leaning against the boxes. "I'll ride; these two can pull."

"In your dreams," said Karl.

"Okay, I'll walk—but only if you promise to read *Murder on the Orient Express*. It's one of Agatha Christie's best." He grinned at President Zander.

"One of these days Zander's going to throw you out of the church," Karl said as soon as we were alone.

"And you along with me," said Helmuth. "But not Rudi. Never Rudi."

"That's not fair. I should be thrown out if you are."

"But you know when to keep your mouth shut," said Helmuth.

Helmuth was right. I never trusted my own opinions, so I usually kept quiet.

"President Zander wouldn't want to get rid of us," said Karl. "He needs us too much. Who'd haul this wagon all over Hamburg for him? Where to, Rudi?"

"Sister Hermann. On Lindenstrasse."

Karl stayed outside to guard the wagon while Helmuth and I climbed the stairs to Sister Hermann's cramped apartment. It was stuffed with sagging, musty furniture, and the tables and walls were completely covered with old photographs. Sister Hermann insisted on introducing us to each picture. I grew impatient, but Helmuth took his time, peering closely at every dark photo and asking questions.

When we got back to the street, Karl was sitting on the sidewalk, leaning against a lamppost. "I was about to call in the Lord Lister detectives. The Case of the Missing Delivery Boys."

"From now on, we'd better leave Helmuth to guard the wagon," I said. "He's too nosy."

"Rudi would rather drop the box by the door, knock, and run," Helmuth said. "That's his idea of Christian charity."

"I would not!"

"Speaking of Lord Lister," Helmuth said, "I'm about to make your lives exciting."

"Delivering food isn't exciting?" Karl asked.

"The police need our help. I've been reading the crime reports in the paper—there are plenty of unsolved cases. We'll make a game out of it."

Karl looked at me. "He thinks he's Sherlock Holmes."

Helmuth smiled. "Maybe I am."

"The police will laugh," said Karl.

"I know a detective—Herr Klaus. He'll listen," said Helmuth. "It's just for fun."

Karl laughed. "So that's why you've been shoving mysteries down my throat. Getting me ready for the Lord Lister Detective Agency."

"That's what we should call ourselves," I said. "What do you think, Helmuth?"

"Sure, Rudi. Okay with you, Karl?"

Karl sighed. "Oh, all right. But I still like westerns better."

"Would you rather play cowboys and Indians?" I asked.

"Very funny," said Karl. "I thought you knew when to keep your mouth shut."

"What happens next?" I asked. "With the Lord Lister Detective Agency, I mean."

"I need to talk to Herr Klaus," Helmuth said.

"I'm ready to start *now*," Karl announced. "I declare the Lord Lister Detective Agency open for business. Our first case—tracking down poor widows!"

He reached for the wagon. Helmuth tried to fight him off, but Karl was bigger and stronger. He jerked the handle away and set off at high speed. "Time is running out," he yelled. "We must find them before it's too late."

"I told you he's crazy," said Helmuth.

We chased Karl down the narrow street, which was crowded with apartment buildings. He weaved around the gas lamps that lined the sidewalk, the wagon tilting precariously. He finally stopped when he reached the corner and needed our help lifting the wagon over the curb.

Our mission took us through several neighborhoods, including Hammerbrook, where Helmuth lived with his grandparents. We weren't far from his street when someone shouted his name. A dozen Deutsches Jungvolk were hurrying toward us.

"Helmuth!" one of the boys called. "Helmuth Guddat!"

Helmuth waved. "Hello, Wilhelm."

It was a warm September day, and the boys wore their summer uniforms: a brown shirt with a swastika patch and neckerchief, black shorts, and, best of all, a dagger. I really liked those uniforms because they reminded me of the Boy Scouts. I never got a chance to become a Scout because Hitler banned them when I was eight. But DJ, the Deutsches Jungvolk, seemed the same, and I wanted to join—except Mutti wouldn't let me.

"I thought you'd have joined by now, Helmuth," said Wilhelm. "You said you'd let me know."

"Still thinking," said Helmuth. "Trouble is, I don't look good in shorts."

Wilhelm laughed. "Membership is now mandatory, so there's nothing to think about. And besides, it's fun. We're off to play war games now. Why don't you come?"

"War games?" Helmuth shook his head.

"This guy must be a Jew," sneered another kid. "Maybe his friends are Jews, too."

"Shut up, Max," said Wilhelm.

Karl dropped the wagon handle, standing to his full height. "Yeah, shut up."

Wilhelm stopped Max, who'd started toward Karl. "We're being friendly," he said. "Come, and bring your friends, too."

Helmuth smiled and shook his head again. He pointed to the wagon. "Sorry, we're busy. Some church work."

Max snorted.

"Karl's already a member," Helmuth continued. "And Rudi will join soon. He wants a dagger like yours."

I stared at Helmuth. How did he know about the dagger?

"But what about you?" asked Wilhelm.

"I'll come Wednesday night," said Helmuth.

"You'd better," Max growled.

Wilhelm shot him a deadly look, but then he said, "In a way Max is right—you *must* come. It's your duty as a German."

Helmuth glanced at Karl and me. I was afraid he might repeat what Brother Worbs had said about Germans and Nazis. Instead he said, "Wednesday night, then."

"Good." Wilhelm motioned to the others. "See you there."

We stood for a moment, watching them march away. Suddenly, Wilhelm stopped, raised his arm, and clicked together the heels of his heavy black shoes. "Heil Hitler!" he said.

Chapter Two

That night I asked Mutti if I could join the DJ. She sighed, then asked me to sit down. "I made a promise to your father," she said.

I looked past her into the kitchen where the box of food from President Zander sat, yet another reminder that Papa was gone. He'd died two years ago, leaving us practically penniless. With help from the church and a job cleaning offices, Mutti kept us afloat. Luckily, Papa had fought in the Great War, and that qualified her for a small pension. Still, it was hard for us to survive.

"What did you promise Papa?"

Mutti didn't answer at first. The room was so still I could hear a streetcar rattling by two blocks away. "Your papa never trusted the

Nazis, right from the start." She lowered her voice. "He called Hitler a criminal. I said he was overreacting. But now . . ."

"But now . . . what?" I asked. Since Hitler had taken over, everyone had a job—we were all eating better. Life was still hard, but it was better than it had been.

Mutti stood and began rearranging figurines on the bookshelf. I watched her without saying anything more.

"It was one of the last things he said to me. 'Don't let Rudi become a Nazi.'" Tears filled her eyes. "Look around you, Rudi! Can't you see what's happening? Herr Beck, your favorite teacher, fired because he's Jewish. Herr Brauer—gone because he wouldn't join the Nazis' Teacher Alliance. The Nazis have passed laws to keep Jews from voting or marrying anyone but a Jew. Your papa was right, Rudi."

I felt my throat close. "I don't want to be a Nazi—I want to be a Boy Scout. It's the law. I have to join. Someday soon they'll make me."

"I know," said Mutti, "but I wanted to keep my promise as long as possible. Papa would understand what we're up against."

"Does that mean yes?"

Mutti nodded.

I kissed her on the cheek and started toward my room. I thought I'd feel happy about getting my way, but instead I felt strangely sad. I looked back at her. She stood at the window, staring into the dark street.

Now that I had permission to join the Deutsches Jungvolk, I didn't care about it as much. Maybe I'd just wanted the right to choose for myself. Or maybe it had to do with my father—knowing how he'd felt about Nazis. Anyhow, I kept putting it off, telling myself every day that I'd join the next day.

True to his word, Helmuth attended the Wednesday meeting and came away a member. "Just to get Wilhelm off my back," he said. That didn't fool me. Helmuth wanted to be a Boy Scout—he'd always liked all the hiking and camping. However, Helmuth and Karl had a problem balancing DJ and church. Both groups held meetings on Sundays and on Wednesday nights.

With school, church, and now the Deutsches Jungvolk, Helmuth was slow getting the Lord Lister Detective Agency on track. I couldn't wait to get started—we'd have so much fun I'd be able to forget DJ altogether. But school made that impossible. More and more boys were wearing their DJ uniforms to class. And I liked their winter outfits even better than the summer ones. Still, I didn't join—until one day in mid-October.

It was a better school day than usual. Our science teacher, Herr Olbricht, took us on a field trip to the Elbe Tunnel. The autumn air was cool and scented with burning leaves—so much better than being in our dingy classroom. The trip took us to the waterfront where all the big ships docked. It was amazing that ocean liners could travel so far up the Elbe River from the sea. The deafening blare of steam whistles, the screaming of gulls, the smell of river water mixed with spices and other exotic aromas, the sight of dark-skinned men unloading straw-baled cargoes from South America or Africa—I loved it all.

When we reached the tunnel, Herr Olbricht smiled and pointed at the entrance. "A product of the superior German scientific mind," he said.

Twin tubes, brightly lit and covered in white tiles, ran underneath the Elbe. Huge elevators inside domed buildings on each bank lifted and lowered automobiles and people from the tunnel openings.

When we returned to school, Herr Olbricht asked if we'd enjoyed the field trip.

"Better than doing math," said Erich Lembeck, and we all laughed—even Herr Olbricht—because Erich was our top math student. He was also one of my best school friends.

"As you saw today, there is little in the world to rival German engineering," said Herr Olbricht. "We can be quite proud of the Fatherland."

Erich held up his hand. "But the English did it first—a tunnel under a river, I mean. And the Americans have built an automobile tunnel that's much longer than ours."

Herr Olbricht nodded curtly. "Yes, that's true. The Holland Tunnel runs under the Hudson River to New York City. But remember, the Americans, except for their Jews and Negroes, are much like we are. And Clifford Holland, its engineer, is of the purest racial background. He is an Aryan, just like us Germans."

I tried to catch Erich's eye, to congratulate him for getting one up on Herr Olbricht, but he wouldn't look at me. Instead, he stared at his hands, clasped tightly in his lap.

"Now, let's see what you learned from today's experience," Herr Olbricht continued. "Take out your notebooks and number a page from one to ten."

After the quiz, Herr Olbricht released us for lunch. Erich and I headed to the school yard to kick around a soccer ball. Others joined us, and soon we had a game going.

When we were called inside, Erich picked up the ball and walked next to me. As we started up the stone steps, he whispered, "Herr Olbricht's wrong, you know. Being a Jew is about religion, not race."

I looked at him in surprise, not knowing what to say.

His serious expression melted into a smile. "I don't think he was going to tell us about the Holland Tunnel, do you?"

I laughed. "Not on your life! He was looking darts at you."

"Darts? More like spears." Otto fell in beside us. "It was hilarious, Erich!"

We joked about Herr Olbricht the rest of the

way to our classroom, but our smiles faded as we walked through the door.

Two Brownshirts in full uniform stood in front, next to a table flanked by two flags—the usual red-and-black Nazi swastika and a black flag with a white eagle. Our teachers were nowhere to be seen.

One of the Brownshirts, a small man with a face like a weasel, was so thin that his swastika armband wouldn't stay up. It slipped down his arm and fell to the floor. No one laughed.

When we'd all taken our seats, the skinny Brownshirt raised his arm and shouted, "Heil Hitler!"

We stood and answered, "Heil Hitler!"

"Be seated," the man said. "I am Baumann, director of the Deutsches Jungvolk in this part of Hamburg. I am here today to sign up those who have not yet joined."

I felt a strange sense of relief—the decision was no longer mine. Erich looked at me, his eyes wide. I didn't know if he was a member or not. For some reason we'd never talked about DJ.

"I will call you up one by one. But before I begin, there is another important matter of business. There are boys among you who do not qualify for membership in the Deutsches Jungvolk. Boys who are a disgrace to the Fatherland. Boys who dishonor the name of our blessed Führer."

The man paused. The room seemed charged with electricity, and our eyes were fastened on him. No one moved a muscle.

"Martin Mann, come forward."

Martin pulled himself to his feet and shuffled to the front, his eyes on the floor.

What is this? I wondered. What's happening? I looked to Erich for an answer, but he was staring straight ahead. Baumann's next words turned me to stone.

"Erich Lembeck. Forward."

Erich and Martin stood next to Baumann. He stepped away from them with a disgusted grunt and strode to the chalkboard. In large letters he wrote, THE JEW IS OUR GREATEST ENEMY.

"Half-Jews!" he said. "Blood tainted by Jewish mothers. Even one drop of Jewish blood makes a boy worthless. The Führer will not allow a Jew to join pure-blooded Germans in the Deutsches Jungvolk. Go home, Jew-boys."

The room was silent as Martin and Erich

gathered their things, careful to look at no one, and walked out the door. I felt sick to my stomach.

"Erich a Jew?" someone behind me whispered.

Baumann smiled. "That's better," he said. "The air is cleaner now."

He sat down and began calling us forward. I slouched in my desk, stunned. Was there really something wrong with Jews? But Jesus was a Jew. My doctor and Erich were Jews. Then I saw myself in a DJ uniform. My father was there. Suddenly, he slapped me hard across the face and ripped the swastika from my arm.

"Rudolf Ollenik."

Otto poked me in the ribs. "Your turn, Rudi."

I jumped up and stumbled to the table.

"Rudolf Ollenik?" Baumann asked.

I nodded. The other Brownshirt checked my name off his list.

"Do you belong to the Deutsches Jungvolk?"

"No sir," I answered.

"Give me ten pfennig for the membership fee, and I will register you now." He held out his hand.

"I don't have ten pfennig."

"We can get your money later. Report on Sunday at ten A.M. A group meets near your place in Rothenburgsort. Here is the address. Congratulations, you are now a member of the Jungvolk."

"I can't come on Sundays," I said. "I have church."

His eyes narrowed. "God and Country go together. Report for duty next Sunday at ten A.M."

Suddenly I wanted to see Helmuth. He was the only one who could make sense of today.

Chapter Three

After school, I rode over to Helmuth's apartment and bounded up the stairs, nearly knocking down his grandmother, who was sweeping the landing.

"Rudi, what's the matter?" she asked.

"Hello, Sister Sudrow. Is Helmuth home?"

"Of course. Come in." She motioned to the door. Delicious smells of baking drifted from inside.

"Helmuth is in his room. Rudi, I believe I baked too much apple tart. Do you know anyone who'd help eat the extra?" Her eyes twinkled. "I'll call you when it's cooled."

Helmuth's door was closed, so I knocked hard twice, then pushed it open anyway. He was completely absorbed in his reading and looked up as I stomped in.

"Rudi! What's wrong?"

I told him about Erich and Martin. I told him about DJ and my father. And then I told him how hard it was for me to understand what was going on.

Helmuth walked over to his window and stared into the deep autumn sky. "Stop it," he said.

I dropped to his bed, too surprised to answer.

"Stop pretending you don't know what's going on. You know exactly what's going on. How many signs did you see today telling you not to buy in Jewish stores? How many of your teachers have suddenly left? How many of your classmates? Face it, Rudi. Nazis are pigs, and Jews are in big trouble."

"But Erich's the best math student. He's good at soccer. And he's funny. Everybody wants to be around him. I didn't even know he was Jewish—no one did. And what about President Zander? He's a Nazi. He's not a pig."

"I believe in the Bible and the Book of Mormon more than I do President Zander," said

Helmuth. "They don't teach us to treat people like that."

"But how can you feel that way about Nazis and join DJ?"

"What choice do we have? You don't want to make trouble for your mother, do you?"

"You think the Nazis would bother her? Because I'm not in DJ?"

Helmuth sighed. "They bothered my mother—first the block leader, then the DJ leaders. That's why I joined. She was worried about losing her job. I didn't tell you or Karl."

Helmuth's mother was also a widow. She had an even harder time than Mutti, which is one of the reasons Helmuth stayed with his grandparents. Another reason was her boy-friend—a Nazi named Hübener. He was an SS man, one of Hitler's elite guard, and Helmuth didn't like him.

"They threatened her?"

"Yes, in a roundabout way. Hans wanted to go after the block leader, but she stopped him."

Hans was Helmuth's older half brother. Helmuth used to share a room with him, but Hans was on his own now. We rarely saw him.

"What about Corporal Hübener?" I asked.

Helmuth's eyes narrowed. "What about him?"

"Did he—" The look on Helmuth's face stopped me.

"Yes!" he said. "It's none of his business! Why doesn't he leave us alone?"

"Boys," Frau Sudrow called from the kitchen. "I need your help. Can you get rid of this apple tart for me?"

At the sound of her voice, Helmuth's anger drained away. I pulled myself off the bed, knowing that I'd decided to join DJ just when I'd decided I didn't want to.

"I've got something to show you," Helmuth said after we finished eating. He dropped a small card on the table in front of me. LORD LISTER DETECTIVE AGENCY, it read. RUDOLF OLLENIK, BADGE NUMBER 2. The card was decorated with a bright drawing of England's flag.

"ID cards. This must mean we're in business."

"That's right," said Helmuth, holding up two more cards. "Helmuth Guddat, Badge Number 1—of course. Karl Schneider, Badge Number 3. You're Number 2 because you always like to be in the middle of things."

"I do not."

"Sure you do. Don't you always take the middle ground when Karl and I argue? Here's a copy of our Code of Conduct."

Helmuth was always good with details. The ID cards looked professional, and the Code of Conduct sounded very official: "Representatives of the Lord Lister Detective Agency pledge to sustain and uphold the law. . . ."

"Let's get started," said Helmuth.

"Now? But Mutti doesn't know I'm here. I should've left a note."

"No excuses," said Helmuth. "Come on. We're going to Eiffestrasse. I want to buy a newspaper and check the police report."

"What about Karl?" I asked.

"Don't worry about Karl. And don't worry about your mother. You'll be home before she is. Here, give me your plate."

Helmuth rinsed our dishes. "That detective I was telling you about said he'd be happy for any leads we can give him. He showed me how to leave him messages at the station."

I wasn't surprised that the detective took him seriously. People always did. Helmuth was a strange mixture of child and adult and could suddenly be either one. He could play like a kid one minute and discuss politics with grown-ups the next. If he wanted the police to listen, they would.

We rushed out the door, nearly running over Helmuth's grandfather, who was making his way carefully up the stairs.

"Hello, Brother Sudrow," I said.

"Good-bye, Grandfather," Helmuth called.

Herr Sudrow pasted himself against the wall in mock terror as we thundered down the steps. Then he laughed and continued his slow upward march. We pushed out into the street and headed toward the shops.

"Criminals beware," I said as we laughed and jostled one another.

We turned the corner that put us on Eiffe-strasse, and the sound of shattering glass brought us to a dead stop. The SA—storm troopers—were smashing the window of Gold-farb's shoe store. They reached through the gaping hole and began flinging shoes and boots out into the street. Black-uniformed SS men stood off to the side, watching.

The brown-shirted storm troopers entered the shop. A chair flew through the window, crashing onto the cobblestones, then boxes, tables, shelves, and even the shop's counter and cash register, littering the sidewalk and street.

"*Juden heraus!*" yelled one of the storm troopers. "You filthy Jews! Get out here!"

From inside the store, a woman screamed. Helmuth took a step forward, but I grabbed his sleeve and pulled him back. We huddled against a building, watching in horror. I looked around for a policeman—someone to help—but that was a stupid idea. The SS and the SA *were* the law.

Without warning, a vanity table flew through an upstairs window. Glass showered the street as the table exploded on impact. The woman screamed again.

I felt Helmuth shivering. I thought he was afraid, until I looked at his face. He was shaking with rage.

"Come on, let's go," I whispered, pulling him forward. But Helmuth pushed my hand away as his eyes locked on one of the SS men. They stared at each other until the man lowered his gaze.

The storm troopers dragged the Goldfarbs—father, mother, and two sons—from the shop and threw them on the cobblestones. Then they began to kick them. The sickening thud of jackboots against flesh and bone was punctuated by muffled grunts and shrill cries.

The SS men waved forward a small group of Hitler Jugend. These boys were sixteen or seventeen and were dressed in the same brown shirts as the storm troopers. They formed a circle around the Goldfarbs, who lay on the cobblestones, unmoving and bloody. Suddenly, they opened the fronts of their trousers, and torrents of urine doused the Goldfarbs. A gasp rose from the crowd that had gathered along the sidewalk.

One of the SS officers stepped forward. "Go! Clean yourselves." His voice was little more than a whisper, yet everyone heard. "Then get ready. We will be back for you." He marched off, followed by the rest of the Nazis.

None of us moved until the Goldfarbs stirred. They pulled themselves to their knees, then struggled to stand. Without looking at anyone, they slowly moved inside, closing the shop's door behind them.

I stared at the door, with its ragged edge of broken glass, while the rest of the crowd moved uneasily around me. No one looked toward the wet stain on the cobblestones, and no one spoke.

When I finally pulled my eyes away from their store, Helmuth was gone. Had he run after the Brownshirts? I headed back the way we'd come and found him walking slowly toward his apartment.

"Helmuth," I called.

He stopped and turned toward me, his eyes moist. "Sorry, Rudi. I thought you were right behind me."

"Helmuth . . . was that Corporal Hübener? The man you stared at?"

Helmuth stiffened. "Don't ever say that name to me again, Rudi. Do you understand? Never."

We walked the rest of the way in silence. I followed him up the stairs, and we let ourselves quietly into his apartment. His grandparents were in their small living room, listening so intently to the radio that they didn't notice we were home.

"Everyone says that Jews control all the money, so they make life hard for the rest of us," I said when we were back in his room.

Helmuth laughed. "The Goldfarbs have

trunks of money hidden under their floor. That's why he sells shoes. So no one will know how rich he is."

"I didn't say I believed that stuff," I answered sullenly.

"It's not just the Jews," said Helmuth. "Remember Herr Braun from upstairs? He refused to take an oath to the Führer. He's a Jehovah's Witness, and it's against his religion. The Gestapo took him away. Maybe Mormons will be next."

I felt cold inside.

"None of us is safe." Helmuth walked to his desk. "See what I found in my math book yesterday?" He handed the book to me. "Look at the fourth problem."

I started to read.

In 1936, the State Welfare Department provided 60,530,575 days of care to institutionalize the mentally ill, blind, deaf, dumb, and crippled.
Assignment:

a) Project the annual expenses for the above patients at a cost of RM 4.501 per day.

b) Compare this enormous annual cost with a day's wages for a worker's time in a production factory. How many days of labor does it take to support these people if an average worker earns RM 3.20 per day?

c) How many workers, with 300 working days per year and an average daily income of RM 3.20, could a factory employ if the state didn't have the burden of supporting these people?

I looked up in surprise.

"Jews, other religions, the blind. Soon they'll be beating up people in wheelchairs. And we'll all stand around watching!" Helmuth grabbed the book from me and flung it across the room. "Or maybe we'll join in!"

I wasn't listening anymore. "My uncle Friedrich is blind," I said.

Chapter Four

Erich didn't come to school the next day. Martin didn't, either. They never came back.

The other boys were still buzzing about yesterday, but I sat quietly, thinking about Erich. Right before class started, my homeroom teacher called me to his desk.

"Rudolf, I was asked to give you this note," Herr Günther said. "Take my advice. Do exactly what they tell you."

"Thank you," I said.

The note was from the Deutsches Jungvolk. The troop leader invited me—though it sounded more like an order—to attend meetings on Sunday mornings and Wednesday evenings. The note also said that I needed to come in uniform—a brown shirt.

I knew Mutti couldn't buy me a shirt on such short notice, so I decided to skip the Sunday meeting. Wednesday evening was easier anyway.

On Sunday morning I went to church as usual. Sunday School started at ten, but Mutti and I always arrived a little early to visit with friends. I looked for Helmuth but only saw his brother, Hans. Karl told me that Helmuth wasn't coming.

"He has DJ duty," Karl said. "Hiking in the country. For that, I'd skip Sunday School, too." His eyes darted to something behind me, and he stopped.

I turned. President Zander was standing near Mutti. He wore a brown shirt and swastika armband.

Karl kept his eyes on Zander. "Helmuth told me about the Goldfarbs," he whispered. "Do you think President Zander gets that kind of SA duty?" Then he said loudly, "So you joined the DJ. Good for you!"

President Zander smiled and came toward us. I felt like kicking Karl.

"Congratulations, Rudi," he said, grabbing

my hand and shaking it hard. "And where is Helmuth?"

"Doing his duty, President," said Karl, clicking his heels together. "On an outing with his platoon."

President Zander's eyes narrowed. "I wish you boys didn't have to miss church for the Jungvolk. But it's one of the sacrifices required of us to return Germany to its greatness." Then he shook Karl's hand, too, and moved away from us to greet other members.

"Thanks a lot," I whispered.

Karl laughed. "I couldn't resist. He's so proud of you, Rudi. You're his favorite little Brownshirt."

"You're not funny," I said.

"Oh, yes I am." He grinned. "But I do have one serious question. How can we believe what Jesus taught and believe in the Nazis, too? How does Zander do that?"

I didn't have an answer.

Mutti was able to pick up a brown shirt before my first DJ meeting. As it turned out, most of the boys from my class were in my platoon, and two of them, Hermann and Werner, were in my squad.

Our leader, Ernst Lang, seemed nice enough, though he was in full SA uniform and flung about "Heil Hitlers" every chance he got. But at least he didn't talk about getting rid of the Jews or killing the Communists. And I think he really liked us.

Wednesday night meetings were called "home evenings," which sounded cozy, and Lang welcomed me warmly. Truth is, I wanted to hate all my Jungvolk experiences far more than I did. Maybe I was so busy pretending to be a Boy Scout that I forgot about the Nazis.

For the next year, Helmuth, Karl, and I saw one another mostly on weekends, though not always at Sunday School because of Jungvolk duty. In spite of this, we kept the Lord Lister Detective Agency alive. We'd check the papers for unsolved crimes, then poke around for clues. Herr Klaus was impressed with Helmuth and encouraged him to keep trying. Karl and I were just tagalongs as far as he was concerned.

Then Karl turned fourteen and moved from DJ into HJ, the Hitler Jugend. Soon after, he finished school and started his apprenticeship as a painter. Suddenly, he was too old for our detective game, but Helmuth and I continued without him.

I turned twelve that year and was finally able to join Helmuth and Karl for MIA. That usually meant missing DJ home evening, but sometimes it was possible to make both meetings by leaving the Nazis a little early or arriving at church a little late. I'd gotten to like DJ a lot, so I tried hard not to miss it—until a new leader took over our troop.

Herr Lang was suddenly gone. No one told us where he went. His replacement, Herr Becher, told us that he'd been transferred. Maybe Herr Lang hadn't been as hardened a Nazi as required.

Becher was a first-rate Nazi. He started in on the Jews during our first meeting. "Feel no compassion for the Jew," he would shout. He even had us play a game called Get the Jews Out! We'd roll dice and move around the board, each boy trying to be the first to throw six Jews out of their houses and send them off to Palestine.

War games became our major activity. Our platoon, sometimes our entire troop, would be divided into two armies to fight each other. We would kill one another by ripping away our colored armbands, but often the weaker boys would be beaten up. Becher encouraged that. "German youth must be as strong as iron," he would say. "They must show no mercy because our enemies will show us no mercy."

One Wednesday night in the autumn of 1938, Becher met with our platoon. We started out by singing the "Horst Wessel Song."

"Raise high the flag!
Close up the ranks tightly!
The SA is marching with quiet, firm tread. . . ."

After singing, we recited the Jungvolk oath: "I promise to do my duty at all times, in love and faithfulness to help the Führer. So help me God." I felt nervous including God in my pledge to the Nazis. Suddenly, I was seeing Erich standing at the front of our classroom. And the Goldfarbs lying in the street. And the page in Helmuth's math book.

"I thought God loved everyone," I said.

Becher slowly turned to me. "What is your point, Rudi?"

"We promise loyalty to the Führer in God's name. Does that mean God is on the Führer's side?"

"Of course! Why are you asking stupid questions?"

I couldn't stop. "Because God loves everyone, so the Führer should, too. But he hates the Jews, and Jesus was a Jew. I don't understand."

Becher's face turned crimson. He slammed his fist against a tabletop. "The Jews *killed* your Jesus!" he screamed. "Christ killers! And for this they were cursed!" He rounded the table and started toward me. "Are you doubting Adolf Hitler? The man God chose to save Germany? You're a Mormon, aren't you?"

I couldn't answer.

Becher thrust his face into mine. "I asked you a question, Ollenik."

The other boys shrank against the walls. "Yes," I whispered.

"A Mormon." Sneering, Becher turned to the other boys. "Watch out for Mormons. They are Jew lovers. I'll have to report this to the Gestapo, if this is how all Mormons think."

"I don't know how other Mormons think!"

What had I done? "What I said about God, that just jumped into my head. No one told me what to think."

"Then stop this now." Becher surveyed the room. "Werner, does your family buy from Jewish shops?" he asked.

"No sir!" Werner answered.

"My father told me that Jews kill Christian babies and use their blood to make Passover bread," said Hermann.

"That's not true," I said, my voice shaking.

Becher rounded on me again. "It's true! All true. Jews seek to destroy all other races. We must protect ourselves against their cunning ways by striking first!"

"I steal from Jewish shops," Hermann said. "And beat up the Jews on our street."

A chorus swelled from the rest of the boys. "Me too! Me too!"

"Good!" said Becher. "But there are other things you can do. . . ."

I stood and started for the door.

"Where are you going, Ollenik?" said Becher.

"My stomach . . ."

"Maybe you'd better go home," he said. "Strong talk upsets weak bellies."

I shook my head. "I just need the toilet."

The other boys snickered.

When I returned, everyone ignored me, except for an occasional sideways glance. Right before the meeting ended, the door opened and Werner slipped into the room. I caught his eye, and he looked away quickly.

Luckily, home evening ended early. If I hurried, I could still make it to MIA. I rushed out and headed for the streetcar stop, images of Becher playing over and over behind my eyes.

I was so angry that I didn't hear the footsteps behind me until it was too late. Hands grabbed my arms, and arms circled my neck. I was hauled off the street into a narrow alley.

"Let go!" I yelled.

"Quiet, Jew lover," Werner whispered. "We've decided to be kind to you. We won't report you and your Mormons to the Gestapo. But you need to be taught a lesson."

Hermann kicked the back of my leg, and I fell to the pavement. Four boys held me down.

"Your church ideas are traitors' ideas," said Werner.

"I told you, those were my *own* ideas."

Werner shrugged. "You need inspiration to help you see the light. So, we're going to give you the Holy Ghost." He nodded to Hermann.

Hermann knelt down and reached for my belt buckle. I yelled until someone slammed his hand over my mouth. I bit him. He slugged me in the teeth, and I tasted blood as he stuffed a handkerchief between my jaws.

They held me tightly as Hermann undid my pants, pulling them and my underwear down to my ankles. Then they rolled me over onto my stomach.

Werner pulled a container of shoe polish from his pocket and opened it. "By the power vested in me by the Church of the Führer, I administer unto you the Holy Ghost!"

Werner smeared the polish on my butt. Then the boys flipped me over, and Hermann also slapped shoe polish on my legs and stomach, even on my privates. Three others took a turn before they released me.

"No more Jew-lover talk from you," said Werner. "The Gestapo won't be so gentle."

I looked away, choking back sobs. When I looked again, the alley was empty. I struggled to my feet, pulling up my pants and brushing dirt from my clothes. Then I stepped into the street and turned toward home.

Chapter Five

"The Church of the Führer?" We were huddled in a corner of the church foyer, and Helmuth struggled to keep his voice low.

I nodded.

"Mocking God is a Nazi pastime. Look at this," he said, pulling a wrinkled scrap of paper from his pocket. Karl looked over my shoulder; we read it together.

Führer, my Führer, bequeathed to me by the
    Lord,
Protect and preserve me as long as I live!
Thou hast rescued Germany from deepest
    distress,
I thank thee today for my daily bread,
Abide thou long with me, forsake me not,

Führer, my Führer, my faith and my life!
Heil, my Führer.

"Where'd you get this?" asked Karl.

"From an eight-year-old kid who lives in my building. Her teachers make her say it every day before lunch."

Karl wadded the paper in his fist.

"Don't be surprised if there's only one church in Germany someday, and it won't be the Catholics or the Mormons or the Lutherans," said Helmuth.

"The Church of the Führer," said Karl, turning to me. "You were stupid, talking to Becher like that. Stupid but magnificent! Maybe getting the shiniest butt in Hamburg was worth it."

"It's not funny," I said. "I'm still black all over, and I've scrubbed myself raw. It hurts to sit."

Karl's smile faded. "No, it's not funny. I'll pay a visit to your friend Werner. And Hermann."

"Then you'd be the stupid one," said Helmuth. "Becher's just waiting for us to retaliate. We need to be smarter when it comes to fighting back."

"What do you know about fighting back?" Karl asked angrily. "You've never been a fighter."

"And you've never been a thinker."

They glared at each other.

"I'm not going back to DJ," I said.

"Don't draw attention to yourself, Rudi," said Helmuth.

Karl snorted. "What's he supposed to do? Join them to beat up Jews?"

"You can't fight back if you're dead," Helmuth said.

"What are you talking about? Hitler isn't going to execute me for kicking in Werner's teeth."

Helmuth shook his head. "Hitler's already taken over Austria, Karl. And the Sudetenland. The rest of Europe is ready for war. And when we're at war, the Nazis won't put up with anything. Werner's teeth might buy you a firing squad."

"So what are you suggesting?"

"We have to get rid of Hitler," said Helmuth.

Karl laughed. "Why didn't I think of that? And so easy."

"Keep thinking small, Karl," said Helmuth. "Let's talk about something else. I'm tired of Nazis. Rudi, I've found a case to investigate."

"I'll leave you children to your games," said Karl.

We watched him walk toward the chapel. When he finally disappeared inside, Helmuth said, "It's a murder case. A barmaid found dead in an alley. Strangled. Her name is Eva Weiss. They found her downtown, not far from City Hall. The beer garden where she worked was close by."

"Was she old?"

"Only nineteen, not much older than we are, Rudi. And she was pretty. Klaus showed me a picture."

"Eva Weiss," I said as a strange wave of sadness swept over me, sorrow for a girl I didn't even know.

Helmuth sensed the change in my mood and gently laid a hand on my shoulder. "She was engaged. Her fiancé had given her a gold necklace with a dolphin-shaped pendant. It was missing."

"So we look for it?" I asked.

"Of course. But Klaus thinks it's too dangerous for us."

"We're just kids, Helmuth. Karl's right, Lord Lister is nothing but a game."

"A better game than DJ," Helmuth said.

The foyer had grown quiet. We looked up. Helmuth froze like an animal caught in the headlights of a car.

A black SS uniform filled the doorway. Corporal Hübener had walked into church with Emma Guddat on his arm. Though Helmuth's mother often worked on Sundays, she came to church whenever she could. But never before had she brought her boyfriend.

Helmuth scooted quickly along the wall, hidden by the small crowd. Before his mother spotted him, he was gone. Moments later, she found me.

"Rudi!" Emma Guddat grasped my hand. "Where is Helmuth?"

This was the first time I'd gotten a close look at Hugo Hübener. He was tall, with pleasant features and penetrating blue eyes. I reminded myself that this man had been on Eiffestrasse.

"Have you seen Helmuth?" she repeated.

"He left. Jungvolk duty," I lied.

"If not at church, then serving the Fatherland. As it should be. I'm Hugo Hübener," said the corporal. He reached for my hand.

His voice was surprisingly gentle. "Rudi Ollenik," I said.

Emma frowned. "Neither of my boys is here. Hans couldn't make it, either."

"I'm sorry we missed Helmuth," said Corporal Hübener. "But I'm glad we came. I grew up Catholic—though I don't attend church anymore."

I didn't know what to say.

Helmuth's mother sighed. "Nice to see you, Rudi. Come on, darling, I want you to meet our church leader, Arthur Zander. You'll like him. He's a Party member."

I just stood there while they talked and laughed with President Zander. I wanted to hate Hübener—and that frightened me. I wanted to hate him, but I couldn't. And that frightened me, too.

Werner made sure the whole school knew what he'd done to me. But I kept quiet. I even went back to DJ meetings. After a while, the boys seemed to accept me again.

During that time, Helmuth and I were together a lot, but he never once brought up Hugo Hübener. Mostly, we talked about Eva Weiss.

We'd patrol the streets near where she'd been murdered. We'd ask questions about the necklace, or we'd poke around in pawnshops looking for it. And we always kept our eyes on women's necks. A few weeks passed, but we didn't have any luck.

One evening in November, Helmuth and I decided to try again. We hadn't seen much of Karl because of his apprenticeship, but when he found out we were headed downtown, he wanted to come—not to look for Eva's necklace, but to be with us.

"We should go to the movies," Karl said. "Forget playing detectives."

"What do you think, Helmuth?" I asked.

"We'll do both," he said.

Suddenly, an explosion turned our heads. A giant bonfire leaped from a side street near our trolley stop. Dark figures circled the flames, feeding the fire with chairs and tables—even stacks of books. Shadows fluttered wildly against the buildings.

We heard the shattering of glass mixed with savage yelling and the roar of the fire. Glass shards snapped under our feet as we hurried toward the blaze. Every window in every Jewish store was smashed—it was the attack on the Goldfarbs multiplied by a hundred.

Crowds had gathered—some people cheering, others turning their heads away. Men dragged Jews into the street and hurled them into the broken glass, kicking and beating them while others flung their belongings into the fire.

"No Brownshirts or SS," Helmuth said.

There wasn't a single Nazi uniform.

Just then an old man stumbled by. Helmuth stopped him. "Why?" he asked.

"Ernst vom Rath is dead—shot in Paris by a Jew. Part of a conspiracy to destroy the Reich. But now the Jews will pay."

The old man moved toward the bonfire.

"Idiot!" Karl yelled.

Helmuth pushed us toward the streetcar stop. "I'm the idiot," he said. "Why didn't I know?"

"Maybe it's better not to know," Karl answered.

"It's always better to know things, Karl."

"I want to go home," I said.

Helmuth nodded. "Sure, Rudi. Let's go home."

People called November 9 the Night of Broken Glass—Kristallnacht. Jewish synagogues and stores in Hamburg and all over Germany were burned or torn apart, mostly by SA and SS dressed in civilian clothes.

Kristallnacht left a pall hanging over us. We couldn't shake it. Helmuth and I didn't feel like playing detectives anymore. And it made attending DJ meetings worse than ever.

Soon it was Christmas, and we all tried to have a decent time—even though Germany seemed on the brink of war. Helmuth's birthday came soon after, on January 8, and I'd scraped together my spare pennies to buy him a gift. I'd found an old copy of the Book of Mormon in a secondhand bookstore. It dated back to the 1800s, and I knew he'd really love it. Karl wanted to split the cost with me.

The bookstore owner agreed to let us have the book for one mark. Helmuth's birthday was on a Sunday, and we planned to give him the book at church. So after school on the Saturday before, when we had saved just enough money, I headed downtown to Herr Frank's bookshop.

When I drew near the shop, I noticed it had a big sign in the window: Aryanized. Herr Frank wasn't around. When I asked for him, the tall thin man behind the counter wrinkled his nose in disgust.

"The Jew is gone. Didn't you see the sign?"

The sign meant Nazis had taken over a Jewish business, but I hadn't put two and two together.

"He . . . he was holding a book for me. An old edition of the Book of Mormon. I . . . we had to save up a mark for it."

The man turned to a shelf, scanning the book spines. "Here it is. Are you a Mormon, then? You'd better watch out. Jews first, Mormons next."

I left the shop feeling rattled and quickly made my way to the streetcar stop. I turned the corner and collided with someone—a street bum. He dropped his bundle, its contents scattering on the sidewalk. I stooped to help pick up his things, but he pushed me away, muttering angrily.

"Sorry," I said. "I should have been watching. . . ."

Suddenly my eye caught the glint of gold—a golden dolphin.

"I'm sorry," I apologized again. "I'm sorry, Herr . . . Herr . . ."

"Seeman. Go away. Leave me alone."

He disappeared down a small side street. For a moment, I thought about running to the police, but I knew I needed Helmuth with me. I hurried to catch a streetcar to Helmuth's, hoping he'd be home. He was, and we were reporting to Herr Klaus within an hour. Four days later, Klaus called us back to the station.

"We brought in Franz Seeman," he told us. "He still had the necklace. Said he found it on the sidewalk. We got the truth finally."

Eva Weiss was the first and last case we ever solved. The darker days that lay ahead finally put an end to Lord Lister, though we still carried our ID cards as a memory of more carefree times.

Chapter Six

The Nazi grip on Hamburg tightened as 1939 marched forward. I don't think anyone felt safe. Hitler made it a crime if you didn't report the tiniest thing that might be treasonous—criticizing Nazi Party leaders, questioning Germany's strength, or even complaining too much. An anti-Nazi joke could get you arrested, and it might be your neighbor or your own relative who reported you.

People began disappearing from apartment buildings along our street, disappearing without a word. Sometimes the Gestapo would make a big commotion hauling someone away. That's how they took Herr Verhaaren, who lived on the fourth floor. Gestapo agents pounded on the Verhaarens' door, so everyone would be sure to hear. Verhaaren's crime was being an "idler." His boss at the munitions factory said he didn't work hard enough and came in late too many mornings. Herr Verhaaren was sent to a concentration camp for "work education."

Things changed in our building after that. Neighbors no longer jabbered to one another on the stairs or by the mailboxes. Even Mutti, who loved visiting, only said hello and moved on. It was dangerous to be too friendly; you might say the wrong thing. It was the same on the streets. You'd see people looking quickly over their shoulders before talking, which soon became known as the "German glance."

I had to be especially careful at school. Even church didn't feel safe. Most of our members hoped to escape the Nazis for a few hours during meetings, but that didn't happen: President Zander ran our branch as if God, church, and Hitler were all in league.

One evening in August, President Zander strolled into the church with a radio under his arm.

"Not again," Helmuth said.

"But it's the leader of the Church of the Führer tonight," said Karl.

"Listening to Hitler is more than I can take."

"Say that to President Zander."

A few minutes later, loud voices pulled us from our corner. We found Brother Worbs and Brother Schmidt waving their arms and yelling at President Zander, who held the front door open. He had a hammer and heavy sheet of paper in his hands.

"This is a house of worship, Arthur!" said Brother Worbs. "How can you post such an ungodly sign?"

"We are all God's children," Brother Schmidt said, his voice rising another notch.

President Zander's sign read: JEWS NOT ALLOWED TO ENTER.

"If we don't go along with the Party," Zander said, "we might not be holding church at all."

"Is that what you want us to believe?" asked Brother Worbs. "That you wear that uniform to protect us from the Gestapo?"

President Zander glanced over his shoulder. "Keep talking like that, and we'll be taken away."

"This is wrong, Arthur," said Brother

Schmidt. "No matter what your reasons. And it's wrong to listen to that radio in church meetings." He turned to Brother Worbs. "But I agree, Heinrich. Don't say such things."

Brother Worbs stomped away while Zander tacked the sign to the door. Brother Schmidt watched silently, then turned and walked into the chapel, shaking his head.

"I'm sorry you had to hear that, boys," said President Zander.

"Take down the sign," Helmuth said quietly. "Don't do this."

"Helmuth, I'm trying to help us survive."

"The price is too high."

President Zander's face darkened. "Be careful," he said. Then, "Congratulations! I hear your mother is remarrying. Too bad Hugo Hübener isn't a Mormon."

Helmuth nodded curtly and walked away. Karl and I followed in surprise. He hadn't told us about his mother.

"Will you move in with them?" Karl asked.

"I'd die first!" Helmuth said.

When we finally joined everyone in the chapel, the opening prayer for MIA was over.

President Zander turned the radio dial until the announcer's voice became clear. The announcer spoke in hushed tones. "The people are gathered here, waiting for the Führer."

Suddenly the crowd in Berlin shouted, "The Führer is coming! The Führer is coming! *Sieg Heil!*" A band began to play the "Badenweiler March."

Hitler's barking voice cut through the applause, and the crowd fell immediately silent. He began ranting about one of his favorite topics, *"Gemeinnutz geht vor Eigennutz"*—the common good comes before an individual's needs. It seemed like he'd never stop, but when he finally finished, three consecutive *"Sieg Heils"* roared from the crowd. The band broke into *"Deutschland, Deutschland über alles"* and then the "Horst Wessel Song."

It was difficult to do religious things after hearing Hitler, but Brother Schmidt went ahead with a lesson. After a few minutes, he stopped.

"Enough," he said, closing his book. "Let's have some fun."

We decided to have a scripture chase—to see who could find verses the quickest.

"And ye shall know the truth, and the truth shall make you free," said Brother Schmidt.

"Right here," said Helmuth, his finger marking the spot. "John, chapter eight, verse thirty-two."

No one else had even opened their Bibles. That's the way it went for the next four verses.

"I give up," said Karl. "Let's try something different." He moved to the window and stood looking out. Suddenly, he leaped straight up, his feet landing on the broad stone sill. "Bet Helmuth can't match that."

Brother Schmidt laughed.

Karl jumped down, and I decided to try.

"No, Rudi," said Brother Schmidt, but I wasn't going to be denied. I coiled myself and leaped. My toe caught on the edge of the sill and I fell forward—through the glass and out into the warm summer night. Helmuth was through the window and by my side in an instant.

My arm was cut deeply, and Helmuth yelled for a bandage while he applied pressure to stop the squirting blood. Brother Schmidt hurried outside with a towel. He wrapped it around my arm and used his belt to slow the bleeding.

My doctor's office was a few blocks away, closer than any hospital. So Brother Schmidt, the only member with a car, bundled me into the backseat and raced to Dr. Löwenberg's. Helmuth and Karl came, too.

When we pulled up, the place was dark. A sign was on the door: THE JEW IS OUT! I looked at Helmuth, suddenly feeling faint.

We sped toward the closest hospital. When we arrived, a doctor ordered the nurses to wheel me straight into the operating room. I was barely conscious, but I remember the doctor chiding me for my carelessness before the anesthetic took me the rest of the way out.

I woke up in a hospital bed with Helmuth and Karl standing over me. As my head cleared, I was surprised to find myself in a private room instead of a ward lined with beds.

"Welcome back, you clumsy ox," said Karl. He was smiling but sounded worried.

"You're lucky to be alive," said Helmuth. "The doctor was worried about a concussion, but you're too thickheaded for that."

I laughed, then clung to the sheets when the room started spinning.

"You'll have to stay overnight, maybe longer," Karl added. "Brother Schmidt went to get your mother."

"What about you?" I asked. "Shouldn't you go home?"

Karl shook his head. "And leave you with all the pretty nurses?"

Before I could answer, two men in long black coats strode through the door.

"Gestapo!" the taller man announced, raising his arm. "Heil Hitler!"

"Heil Hitler," we mumbled.

"Would you explain this?" the shorter agent asked, holding something toward me. It was my Lord Lister ID card.

Without waiting for my answer, he demanded to see Helmuth's wallet, and Karl's. Karl didn't have his card, but Helmuth did.

"An English group," said the taller man. "What sort of subversive group is this?"

Helmuth laughed. "It's a kids' game—a detective club. We've outgrown it."

The shorter agent stepped close. "Tell the truth. Who are these people?"

He must have thought he could trip me

up more easily because I was still groggy from the anesthetic. His gloved hand grasped my chin.

"Please," I pleaded. "It's just a game."

The agent stepped back, motioning to Karl. "Leave the room," he said.

Karl backed out.

"Take Guddat to the next room."

Suddenly I was alone with him. He stared at me without saying a word. Then without warning, he slapped my face.

"I want the truth. What is your connection to England?"

Tears filled my eyes. Again and again I tried to explain about the Lord Lister mysteries and playing detective, but all I got were slaps.

The other man returned and called his partner into the hall. It grew quiet. The Gestapo agents were suddenly gone.

Helmuth had convinced his interrogator to call Herr Klaus, who immediately verified our story. I'd been too scared to think of that.

Afterward, we wondered why the Gestapo had bothered with us. For days, I couldn't keep myself from worrying about them and watched over my shoulder wherever I went. Then suddenly the whole world changed. On September 1, Hitler attacked Poland; England and France immediately declared war on Germany.

The war made me forget my scare. But only because I didn't know that we now had a permanent Gestapo record—a record that would come back to haunt us.

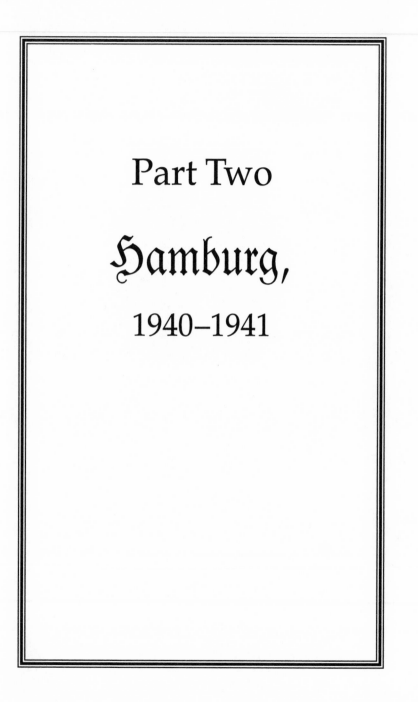

Part Two

Hamburg,

1940–1941

Chapter Seven

It took less than a month to smash Poland, and then our troops returned home. Within a few weeks they were sent to the west, and we waited for fighting to start. But nothing happened. The army just sat there, and we all began hoping for peace. Maybe with Poland conquered, that would be that. Maybe the Führer had all the room he needed for Germany to grow. But Helmuth seemed to know better. "It's the calm before the storm," he said.

Sure enough, the British and French wouldn't listen to Hitler's peace offer. German submarines started attacking British ships.

Soon we were into 1940 and facing changes brought on by the war. Rationing, for instance. It had already been hard to get some sorts of food, but the new rationing laws made it much harder. Even basic necessities required government ration stamps—blue ones for meat, orange for bread, white for sugar, green for eggs—and then shops often didn't have enough to go around. We even had trouble getting things like soap and coal—our apartment was never really warm that winter.

In March, Helmuth's mother married Corporal Hübener, but Helmuth continued to stay with his grandparents. He was still refusing to talk about his new stepfather when Hitler gave the order to invade Denmark and Norway in April. Denmark fell in four hours.

"This isn't much of a war," I said.

It was late on a warm May afternoon. Helmuth and I had poked around in the open-air market that surrounded the giant Nikolai Church, then we'd walked over to Alster Lake. We were killing time until we met Karl at the movies.

"Disappointed?" Helmuth asked. "Were you hoping for a bigger, better war?"

"I didn't mean it that way," I said.

Helmuth stopped and leaned on a rail. He looked out over the lake. Swans floated lazily among canoes and rafts and other boats. Cafés lined the shore, and gulls circled the waterfront, landing on scraps of food.

"Seems too peaceful," he said. "Is that what you mean?"

"I guess so."

"Don't worry. A bigger, better war is on its way."

"Let's change the subject," I said. "No more school!"

"School wasn't so bad, Rudi. I'll miss it."

I'd just graduated and would begin a metalworking apprenticeship with Christian Bolte and Sons, though I'd still be taking a few technical classes. Helmuth was going to be an apprentice with the Hamburg Social Services Department.

Unlike me, Helmuth loved school. He should have been going on, preparing for the university. Helmuth had received the highest mark possible on his final examination essay—something about politics and history that I couldn't come close to understanding. But going to university took a lot of money. Or knowing the right people. Helmuth never had a chance.

We turned away from the lake and started through the streets. A Hitler Jugend patrol stepped around the corner, marching in formation. People on the sidewalk stopped, raising their arms in the Hitler salute. Several boys weaved through the crowd, watching for anyone not saluting.

An old man shuffled from the door of a shop and started down the sidewalk. Instantly, one of the HJ rushed forward, swinging his club. He pounded the old man across the shoulders, hurling him to the pavement.

Helmuth rushed over, and I followed.

"Up, old man!" the boy yelled.

"Leave him alone," said Helmuth.

The HJ raised his club again, but Helmuth didn't flinch. "You're a coward," he said.

For a moment the boy looked stunned, then new fire burned in his eyes. "Weakling!" he yelled, backing away.

A handful of people quietly touched Helmuth's shoulder as they passed, or dipped their heads in his direction. I helped him get the old man up. We took him to his apartment before hurrying to meet Karl.

* * *

A few days later, Hitler marched on France. Not long after, the bigger, better war came to our doorstep. Or maybe I should say to our docks. Hamburg's shipyards were attacked by British bombers, and everyone was surprised. Germany's air force was supposed to be so powerful that no enemy planes could ever get through.

City parks were dug up to make bomb shelters, and rationing worsened. Yet normal life went on, in an odd sort of way. The three of us managed to catch a film or go to a dance or do something together at least one evening a week. And we seldom missed church these days, which meant our attendance at Hitler Jugend meetings was spotty—just enough to keep us on the rolls.

However, the Führer made getting together at nights difficult when he insisted on a new curfew law. No one under eighteen was supposed to be on the streets after dark, except with an adult. Helmuth came up with a way to beat the curfew: "dressing old." Donning homburg hats, overcoats, and silk scarves and carrying umbrellas, we made ourselves look over eighteen.

This worked for the movies, too. Another law kept anyone under eighteen from seeing films with kissing or dancing. One night Helmuth decided we should go to *Jud Süss*, a movie we weren't old enough to see.

Helmuth checked us over, nodding with approval. "Rudi, you look eighteen, no problem. And Karl even older. I'm the problem, being so short."

"You look and act old enough to be our father," Karl said.

Helmuth laughed.

We walked downtown. Along the way, city workers had roped off a crater in the street. The front of a nearby apartment building was ripped off, and windows all along the street were shattered.

"Last night's bombing," said Helmuth.

"We must be imagining this," said Karl. "Göring promised us that not *one enemy plane* would fly over Germany."

"Oh, he'd never break his promise," Helmuth said. "We bombed ourselves, of course."

"A brilliant plan!" Karl slapped his forehead. "I see it clearly now. We bomb ourselves, blame England, England feels bad and calls off the war."

"And to make up for hurting our feelings,

they let us have all of Europe," Helmuth added. "Who said Hitler was stupid?"

I laughed. "I think *you* did."

"Me?"

As we drew near the damaged building, our smiles faded. It was eerie peering into the apartments, stripped open to the evening air like a dollhouse. No one was there, and anything worth taking was gone. Still, I felt like I was prying into private places and turned away.

"Will the bombing get worse?" I asked.

"If the Americans join the war, everything will get worse," said Helmuth.

"Do you think they will?" asked Karl.

"Sooner or later," Helmuth answered. "They're already sending supplies to England. The good news is that Hitler can't win a war against England *and* America."

The thought of fighting against America had never entered my mind. Our church headquarters was there, in Salt Lake City. Fighting America would be like fighting the church.

The sun was setting as we reached the theater. No one seemed to wonder if we were old enough to be out after dark. As it turned out, fourteen-year-olds could go to *Jud Süss* if they were with an adult. We strode in confidently on our own. At least, Helmuth and Karl were confident. I nearly lost my nerve, but Karl wouldn't hear of it. Instead, he pushed money into my hand and forced me toward the box office to buy our tickets.

The film was set in the sixteen or seventeen hundreds. The villain was a Jew named Süss Oppenheimer. He was like the devil, using his money to make life miserable for everyone he met. All the way through I could hear people around me muttering, but when he attacked the pretty blond heroine—who surrendered to him so that her imprisoned husband wouldn't be tortured—angry rumbling filled the theater. Then the entire crowd stood and cheered when he was killed. I jumped up, too.

Helmuth jerked me back into my seat, his mouth a thin line.

As we left the theater, we overheard a few HJ in the crowd planning to find some Jews and make trouble, echoing a line from the film: "May the citizens never forget this lesson."

Helmuth pulled us into a restaurant. He picked the most secluded table, and we sat without talking until the waiter brought our drinks.

"Hard to keep from cheering when they killed Süss Oppenheimer, wasn't it?" Helmuth asked.

"He was just so bad," I said. "I couldn't help it."

"I got so caught up in the story that I almost hated Jews," said Karl.

"Nazi mind control at its best. You heard the crowd...."

"A lot of them already felt that way," said Karl. "All the film did was add wood to the fire."

"It backed up everything we hear about Jews in Jungvolk and HJ," Helmuth said.

"How can we be like this?" Karl asked. "Hitler tells us something and we automatically believe it."

"All we hear is Hitler!" Helmuth whispered fiercely. "No one else. You'd better hope the British win this war."

Chapter Eight

New Year's Eve 1940 found the three of us in a room atop the warehouse complex near our church. Our branch shared in a volunteer air-raid watch, and this spot was used as the watchtower. We'd been assigned by President Zander to spend the night watching for enemy bombers. Our old Sunday School teacher, Heinrich Worbs, agreed to stay with us.

"What a way to spend New Year's Eve," Karl said. He'd wanted to go to a dance with a new girl in the branch.

"Forget Greta," said Helmuth. "We've got everything we need for a party of our own. Food. Games. A radio. I'll even dance with you, if you get lonely." He fluttered his eyes.

Karl rolled his.

"And Brother Worbs can tell ghost stories," I said. He'd been frightening us with his stories since I could remember.

Brother Worbs's eyes lit up. "Don't think I can't scare you, just because you're nearly grown up. You'll be begging me to stop."

"All right," Karl said. "Ghost stories sound good. But don't turn on any music. Please! It might give Helmuth ideas. . . ."

We sat in the dark, keeping an eye on the windows, watching for the Royal Air Force. Brother Worbs told his creepy tales for a couple of hours. "Stop! Stop!" we'd yell after each one, but he'd only laugh and go straight on to another. It was so much fun, we forgot all about the food we'd brought. Karl even forgot about Greta. Finally, as midnight approached, we went up to the roof to welcome in the New Year.

From every corner of Hamburg church bells began to ring. Then steam whistles and fog-horns from the harbor joined in, celebrating the arrival of 1941. Suddenly, fireworks exploded in the sky. They streaked upward from different parts of the city, peppering the darkness with bright colors.

81

Helmuth laughed. "That's Hamburgers for you. War, rationing, blackouts—nothing stops a celebration."

"The Gestapo must be going crazy," said Karl.

The illicit fireworks stopped almost as soon as they'd begun—no one wanted to be tracked down by the police. Still, we were all happier for those few moments.

While Brother Worbs laid out our food, Helmuth fiddled with the radio dial. He was trying to find a foreign station and finally tuned in to Radio Switzerland.

"If we had a shortwave," Helmuth said, "we could pick up England."

"They're illegal," said Karl. "That means any good Gestapo member will have a couple of them at home. We could ask to borrow one sometime. You know how generous the Gestapo are."

Helmuth laughed. "If we're polite, we should be able to get it for a week or two."

"And if we wear our HJ uniforms," Karl added. "So they'll know what good Aryans we are."

"And if the Gestapo ask us why we want a shortwave, we'll tell them the truth—to listen to the BBC. But only to prove the English are liars."

"That'll work," said Karl.

I interrupted at this point. "Don't give him any ideas, Karl. He just might go ahead and do it." I turned to Helmuth. "Of course, how would you be able to find the BBC if you can't even find a station with some decent music?"

He flipped the dial again and a waltz drifted from the speaker. Karl made a big show of backing away from Helmuth, who held out his arms for a dance.

"Decent music, Helmuth!" I said.

"Food's ready," Brother Worbs called from across the room. "Let us bless it and pray for better times."

We bowed our heads.

"Our dear Father in heaven," he began. "We are thankful for our blessings. Thankful that the bombs did not fall this night. Thankful for our faith in thee. And thankful for the food we are about to partake of, and we ask thee to bless it." Brother Worbs paused and then his voice rose. "Give us peace, dear Lord. Break the yoke of the Nazi butchers and make us free so that thy kingdom might roll forth in Germany. In the name of Jesus Christ, Amen."

"Amen," we said, looking nervously at one another. This was the same old Brother Worbs who'd challenged President Zander about the Gestapo.

"Brother Worbs, be careful what you say about the Nazis," said Helmuth. "You don't know who you can trust."

Brother Worbs looked at him. "I tell the truth and only the truth," he said.

Brother Worbs had prayed for peace in the New Year, but 1941 didn't get a peaceful start. Two weeks after New Year's, we were wandering down the hall after Sunday School when Mutti descended on us, prodding us back into our empty classroom.

"They've arrested Brother Worbs," she whispered.

"Someone must have turned him in," said Helmuth.

Mutti shook her head. "The city put up a new statue—a Nazi hero. When they unveiled it, Brother Worbs was there. He said, 'Another monument to the Nazi butchers.' The Gestapo grabbed him right off the street."

She reached out for me. "I'm scared the Gestapo will ask you questions. They have a long memory."

"You mean the Lord Lister problem?" I asked. "Mutti, that was over a year ago."

"You don't know how they think, Rudi," she said.

"We can handle it," said Helmuth.

Mutti was frantic. "But they sent him to a concentration camp. I couldn't live if that happened to you."

"He's nearly seventy," Helmuth whispered. "He'll never make it."

Mutti hugged each of us before we left the room. "Promise me you'll be careful," she said.

President Zander stopped us on our way out of the church. "I can see by your faces you've heard about Brother Worbs. I'm sorry. I know how you feel about him."

"How do *you* feel about him?" Helmuth asked.

"Come on, boys," Mutti said. "We need to be going."

"He's an old friend," said President Zander. "We've disagreed a lot, but that doesn't change how I feel. I want him back, but he'll have to come back wiser. He can't be allowed to put us all in danger."

"Not wiser," said Helmuth. "More afraid, like the rest of us."

"More prudent," said President Zander. "We are at war, Helmuth. We must be united to survive."

"Will Brother Worbs come back?" I asked.

The president's voice softened. "I hope so. Remember him in your prayers."

Mutti pushed us out the door and down the sidewalk. "Helmuth, you already broke your promise," she scolded. "President Zander is a Nazi. How could you talk to him like that?"

Helmuth said, "You used to think he was a good man."

"In many ways, he's still a good man," she said. "He's always helping people."

"Unless you're a Jew," said Helmuth.

"He does have some blind spots," said Mutti. "Blind spots that lead him astray. Watch what you say around him."

"That's what you said to Brother Worbs," I pointed out.

"Ouch," said Helmuth. "But Zander's such a mystery—he's like two different people. He's able to put aside his beliefs the minute he needs to."

"Maybe he adjusts them," Mutti said. "Perhaps he believes he's doing the right thing."

"Then he's lying to himself," said Helmuth.

"Maybe," said Mutti. "But promise me you'll be careful. Please?"

We promised.

These two sides of Zander's personality showed up the very next Sunday. We were all standing around visiting before services when his voice rose above the peaceful murmuring.

"What's this?" he shouted. "Enemy lies!"

Sister Haase, one of our older members, cowered in front of him. He had snatched a paper from her hand and was waving it in her face. It was one of the thousands of leaflets dropped on Hamburg by British airplanes.

"It was on the sidewalk," she whispered. "I was just curious. That's all."

"I won't tolerate this. If you ever bring enemy propaganda into this church again, you'll go to a concentration camp. Do you understand?"

Sister Haase began to sob.

"How could you say that to her?" asked Brother Schmidt.

President Zander flushed. "We don't want the Gestapo thinking we're sympathetic to the enemy."

He looked at us. "We're being watched. Our headquarters is in America," he said. "We can't afford this."

Helmuth and Karl didn't stay for church that day. Mutti wouldn't let me follow them.

That summer, Hitler attacked Russia. Now we were at war on two fronts. That same summer also brought news about Brother Worbs.

"Look who's back!" Karl pointed to a small figure hobbling toward the church. It was Brother Worbs himself.

I was shocked by the haunted look on his face, a face so thin I barely recognized him. Brother Worbs was old when he was taken away, but now he seemed ancient.

We helped him to a small park. The June evening was filled with the warm smells of summer, and the sun was still high above the buildings as we settled onto the benches.

"What did they do to you?" Karl demanded.

Brother Worbs paled. "Quiet!"

Helmuth knelt down and gently took his hand. "Will you tell us what happened?" he asked, his voice so soothing that it broke through the old man's reluctance.

"I've signed a paper. So I must say I was in camp for 'educational purposes' and was treated well. That is my only allowed answer." He noticed the park's new addition—a small bomb shelter. "British bombs are less frightening," he whispered.

We turned the talk to happier times—the laughs on New Year's Eve, the ghost stories he'd scared us with. Brother Worbs barely smiled.

"I was foolish not to listen to you," he said, beginning to tremble. "They tied me up. They forced me to stand naked in the snow." His voice broke. "They poured water over my hands. When it froze, they beat the ice away with a rubber hose. 'To warm them up,' they said."

Helmuth massaged his ruined hands tenderly. I looked away, hiding my tears. A few minutes later, Helmuth helped Brother Worbs to his feet and guided him to the church.

When we walked in with Brother Worbs, a silence descended upon the room. Then someone started to clap, and the place erupted with applause. Brother Schmidt embraced him, and one after another, the other branch members did the same—even President Zander.

He came to life before our eyes that morning, so we never suspected he'd already lost the battle. Five weeks later Heinrich Worbs was dead.

Chapter Nine

After hearing Brother Worbs's story, Helmuth changed. Only Karl and I, who knew him so well, noticed. He became a clerk for President Zander, typing and filing letters. He also stopped saying anything about the Nazis, and he never mentioned the war. On top of these things, Helmuth started to avoid Karl and me. Then, not long after Brother Worbs's funeral, he asked us over to his place.

Karl and I both arrived at nine P.M. We hardly recognized each other in the dark street, since we were "dressed old." Helmuth was waiting for us on the landing. He moved us into his room quickly and closed the door. The place was scattered with books.

"Rob a library?" Karl asked.

"At gunpoint," Helmuth answered with a smile.

One of the books was *Spirit and Action* by Heinrich Mann. I'd never read anything by him, since the Nazis had banned his work.

"Where did you get that?" I pointed at the book, afraid to touch it.

"Where'd you get all of these?" Karl shuffled through them. "Every one is off limits. I thought they were burned."

"They were," Helmuth said.

"So how did you . . . You've been making book runs to Switzerland!"

Helmuth laughed. "Your first guess was closer."

"Robbing libraries?"

Helmuth nodded. "There's a collection of banned books where I work."

"At Social Services? You're stealing books from Social Services?" I asked.

"Borrowing," said Helmuth.

"That's a relief!" Karl said. "The Gestapo would be upset if you were *stealing* them. But *borrowing* illegal books—that's fine by them."

"I'm careful."

"Are you out of your mind?" Karl asked.

"I know what I'm doing. I usually take one at a time, but they're moving the collection and everything is in a mess. I wanted to show them to you."

"Thanks for thinking of us," said Karl. "We thought you'd forgotten who your friends are. You'd rather spend time with Zander than us."

"Well, Zander has such a delightful personality."

Karl laughed. "You're right. We could never compete."

"Why so many books?" I asked Helmuth. "Is this why we haven't seen much of you lately?"

"Partly. Take a look at some of this stuff."

Karl picked up *All Quiet on the Western Front*. "I've always wanted to read this, but never got a chance."

I was still looking at the Heinrich Mann book. "You've read all of this?" I asked.

Helmuth nodded.

"What's it about?"

Helmuth riffled through the pages, thinking what to say. "Heinrich Mann believes that

Germans go after personal security above anything else. Because of that Germans aren't willing to overthrow a bad government—we don't think it would make any difference."

"So Hitler's here to stay," said Karl. "The Nazis should like that idea."

"But *Spirit and Action* is telling us to wake up," Helmuth said. "If Germans listened to Heinrich Mann, we'd get rid of Hitler."

"Hitler and his worshippers," I said.

"If that happened, there'd only be about a hundred people left in Germany," said Karl. "The trouble is, we've let it go too far. There's nothing we can do now."

"We won't know until we try," said Helmuth.

"Try what?" Karl asked. "Who's going to take on the Gestapo?"

"If enough of us join together . . . But people have to know the truth first, and I have something to help with that."

Helmuth opened a cabinet and pulled out a shortwave radio from under some blankets.

Karl whistled softly. "Where'd you find that?" He turned to me. "Don't tell me he actually borrowed one from his friendly neighborhood Gestapo agent!"

"This is real, Karl. Hans got it in Paris. He asked me to hide it for him."

Hans had served in the National Labor Service in France. He hadn't been home for two days when he was drafted into the army and had to leave again.

"It's a Rola," said Helmuth. "A really fine piece of equipment. You can pick up England with no problem."

"England?" I was stunned. "You've been listening to England?"

"The BBC."

"Do your grandparents know?" Karl asked.

Helmuth snorted. "Of course not. Here, listen."

He plugged in the Rola and doused the lights—somehow the darkness made us feel safer. Our faces glowed faintly in the dim light of the radio dial. We heard French voices, and maybe Swedish. Finally, Helmuth settled on a station where the announcer was speaking English. At exactly 10:00 P.M., the first bar of Beethoven's Fifth Symphony trumpeted from the speaker.

"The BBC London presents the news in German."

The newscaster's German pronunciation was perfect. Helmuth scooted close to the lighted dial to write in a notebook.

Most of the report was about the Russian front. German radio and newspapers had been crowing about our great victories as the Wehrmacht marched into the Soviet Union. We'd been told that the Red Army was finished.

But the BBC told a different story. Russia's stubborn resistance was giving Germany trouble. Though Soviet losses were still much higher than German losses, their army was anything but defeated. I wondered if this was just more propaganda, but somehow what the man from the BBC was saying simply rang true.

When the program ended, the announcer gave the times of rebroadcasts and reminded us to change the dial so we wouldn't be caught breaking the law—you could get a death sentence for listening to foreign news. When Helmuth flicked on his lamp, I noticed his notebook page was full.

"Why the notes?" asked Karl. "This isn't school. Besides, it's risky."

Helmuth looked more serious than I'd ever seen him. "This *is* school. Only we're the teachers."

"What are you talking about?" I asked.

"Everyone thinks we'll take Russia by the end of 1941—that the war will be all but won. It isn't true, and we need to let people know."

Helmuth reached under his bed and pulled out a stack of red papers, handing one to each of us. The small rectangles were topped with black swastikas, followed by:

Down with Hitler———
People's Seducer
   People's Corrupter
   People's Traitor
Down with Hitler———

"You've gone over the edge," Karl whispered.

"Think of Brother Worbs. And the Jews. Help me do this, Karl. Help them."

"I'll help," Karl said slowly. Very slowly.

"Rudi?"

"Yes," I whispered.

Helmuth smiled. "This is only a trial run. Next time I'll use news from the BBC. All you need to do is put them in people's mailboxes."

"Where'd you get the swastika stamp?" I asked.

"It's an old one from work. They'll never miss it," said Helmuth.

"You aren't typing these at work, are you?" asked Karl.

"President Zander let me bring the church's typewriter home. I convinced him I could get more done that way."

Karl laughed. "A double agent. He worms his way into Zander's inner circle, then comes away with the ultimate weapon—a typewriter!"

"The typewriter is mightier than the sword, you know." Helmuth smiled.

"Maybe, but is it mightier than the tank?"

"Or the bomber?" I added.

"Absolutely—unless you run out of paper," said Helmuth. "Actually, my biggest problem is speed. If it weren't for carbon paper, I'd never get enough of these finished. Luckily, four leaflets fit on one sheet, and I can type three sheets at a time."

"But why *red* paper?" I asked.

"Beggars can't be choosers," he answered. "I took what was handy."

"From the church?" asked Karl.

Helmuth nodded. "I think God understands. Besides, that paper sat at the bottom of a drawer for years."

"When do we get rid of these things?" I asked.

"We'll do it tonight. Put them in apartment mailboxes or post them in telephone booths. Don't go back to the same places next time. People might remember you." Helmuth seemed on fire.

"How many do you have?" asked Karl.

"Sixty," said Helmuth. He counted out stacks of twenty each.

The deep red paper was the color of blood.

Chapter Ten

We put on our coats and went downstairs. Helmuth started up the street and disappeared into the night.

I pushed my bicycle along as Karl and I walked away. Neither of us said anything.

As soon as Karl left me, I mounted the bike and sped toward Rothenburgsort. The leaflets felt like they were burning through my coat. I heard footsteps running toward me; I jumped at every shadow. But no one stopped me.

I parked my bike at home, then went into a different building on Hardenstrasse. Feeling like a thief, I crept over to the bank of mailboxes and began dropping in the flyers. My hand shook like a branch in the wind.

When I finished there, I tried the next apartment house, hugging the side of the building so that no one would see me. Just as I reached for the door handle, a man burst through the doorway, and my heart nearly exploded. But he ignored me, hurrying away down the sidewalk. I skipped that place and tried a building on the next block.

Finally, I'd rid myself of all the leaflets and was headed home with a bounce in my step. Rushing around the corner onto Hardenstrasse, I nearly bumped into two policemen.

I raised my arm in salute and called out "Heil Hitler!" in my lowest-sounding voice.

"Heil Hitler!" they returned.

Once again, "dressing old" had saved me from being arrested for curfew violation. But what if I'd been stopped? What if I'd been stopped earlier when the leaflets were still in my pocket? My knees began to rattle against each other. As I stood leaning against the wall, my legs weak, I couldn't keep a song out of my head.

The old rotten bones of the world are quaking
About the Great War.

We have broken the bonds of servitude;
For us it was a great victory.
We march on and on,
Even if all is destroyed;
For today Germany shall hear us,
And tomorrow the entire world.

If the Nazis marched on and on, even if everything was destroyed, why bother with the leaflets? I smiled, realizing I was thinking like one of Heinrich Mann's Germans. Suddenly, I was amazed by what I'd just done. How had I dared? The answer was Helmuth. I always listened to him. I trusted him.

I hid in a doorway for a while, until my legs would work again. Then I made my way home. Luckily, Mutti was asleep when I got in—she didn't seem to worry much when I was with Helmuth—and I didn't have to explain why I was so late.

As I lay in bed, I felt myself weaken. Images of Brother Worbs's broken fingers kept me awake, and my confidence turned to fear. I vowed never to help Helmuth again, even if he thought it was the right thing to do.

Even if it *was* the right thing to do.

* * *

The next evening was MIA. Karl and I were in the foyer when Helmuth walked in, looking smug.

"Karl. Rudi. Where have you been?" Helmuth asked. "Why don't you come see me? How about Sunday?"

I gave Helmuth a funny look, but Karl just laughed. "Sure," he said, "we'll be there."

That Sunday evening, Karl and I waited while Helmuth did some work for President Zander. Then we followed him home. He was clutching something under his suit coat.

"What are you hiding?" I asked.

Helmuth pulled out a sheaf of paper.

When we reached the apartment, the Sudrows were already in bed. Helmuth quickly set up the shortwave for the BBC report.

The newscaster announced that one and a half million German soldiers had been killed on the Russian front. Even though our armies were getting close to Moscow, the fighting was fiercer than ever.

"And Hitler says our losses are light," said Helmuth.

The Russian casualties were still much

higher than ours. The totals were up from the last report. Then, to our surprise, the announcer began talking about Rudolf Hess.

Rumors had been going around that Hess had disappeared, but no one knew for sure. Early on, he had been Hitler's right-hand man. Now others, such as Heinrich Himmler and Hermann Göring, were more important, though Hess was still the Deputy Führer. To our amazement, the BBC reported that Hess had flown to Scotland, parachuted from a small plane, and been arrested.

The report ended with the usual warning to change the dial setting, which Helmuth did immediately.

"Hess is crazy," said Karl.

"Did he really believe he could make peace with England?" I asked.

Helmuth shrugged. "Who knows? The British aren't buying it."

"So he did disappear," I said. "The rumors are true."

Helmuth put the radio away, then reached under his bed and pulled out some leaflets.

I groaned. "Not red paper again."

Helmuth ignored me, counting the leaflets into equal piles. I quickly read the top copy.

WHO IS LYING??????????????

```
The official Report of the German
High Command of the Armed Forces.

Quite a while ago they claimed
the roads to Moscow, Kiev
and Leningrad were open.

And today—six weeks after
Germany's invasion of the USSR—
severe battles are still occurring
far from
these places.

This is how they are lying to us!

THIS IS A CHAIN LETTER, SO PASS IT ON!
```

"Listen," said Karl. "I know we're all being careful, but if any of us should get caught, let's make a pledge."

"What do you mean?" I asked.

"If I get caught, then I agree to take all of the blame," said Karl. "How about you two?"

I looked at Helmuth, who was nodding, and tossed aside my vow not to help him.

"Okay," I said, sounding braver than I felt. "I'll do the same."

"Good," said Helmuth. "That way whoever's left can carry on."

We shook hands.

"Come see me." Karl and I heard this every week now. Sometimes we'd stop by on weekdays, sometimes on Sundays, sometimes both. And on the days in between, Helmuth continued to listen to the BBC. He made sure he filled us in on the broadcasts we missed.

Helmuth's third leaflet came straight from the second BBC broadcast we'd heard together. "Altogether, one and a half million German and Austrian soldiers lost their lives," it said about the fighting in Russia. "For that you can thank Hitler!!!!!"

Several days after that, Helmuth had us delivering the next handbill. It told about Rudolf Hess's flight to England. By the first week of September, he'd finished his fifth handbill. When I read it, I couldn't help thinking how the Gestapo would fry us if we were caught.

HITLER IS THE SOLE GUILTY ONE!!!!

By means of the unlimited war in the air, several hundred thousand defenseless civilians have been killed.

But the R.A.F. is not to blame for these killings. Their flights are only in reprisal for the raids of the German Air Force over Warsaw and Rotterdam, where unarmed women and children, cripples and old men were killed.

THIS IS A CHAIN LETTER, SO PASS IT ON!

I wondered afterward if passing out a leaflet about air raids jinxed me. I was several blocks from home, frantically stuffing handbills into mail slots, when air-raid sirens began wailing through the darkness. Searchlights pierced the skies, bright blades slashing back and forth. The British planes, caught in the light, looked tiny and harmless, like moths hovering around a candle—a peaceful image instantly shattered as bombs exploded near the harbor. Then the anti-aircraft guns began spitting streaks of fire, their racket filling the streets.

The dancing lights and the scream of falling bombs almost hypnotized me. I finally snapped to and realized I was standing in the middle of the street holding the leaflets as an air-raid warden ran toward me.

It was illegal to be outside during a bombing attack, and air-raid wardens patrolled the streets, hurrying people along. "Idiot!" the man screamed. "Get underground."

I stuffed the rest of the leaflets into my coat pocket and started to run, but he caught my arm.

"Let me go!" I shouted. "I've got to go home and get my mother. She can't walk."

"No!" He began pulling me toward the shelter, then suddenly stooped to pick up something from the pavement. A leaflet! My heart jumped into my throat as his eyes traveled to my pocket, where two more leaflets dangled.

"What's this?" His grip tightened on my arm.

Suddenly, the warden's hand was gone from my sleeve. He lay sprawled on the cobblestones, his face covered with blood. Anti-aircraft guns were firing at planes directly overhead, and fragments from the bursting shells rained down on the street. A large piece of flak had struck him in the head.

Tiny fragments pelted me, stinging like fire as I pulled him into a nearby doorway. He was still breathing, so I staunched his blood with a handkerchief. I waited a few moments longer until the flak lessened, then bolted for home, the leaflets clutched in my hand.

"It was dark. You were wearing a hat," said Helmuth. "You're safe, Rudi." We were sitting in his room the evening after the air raid.

Karl laughed. "Besides, the poor guy probably woke up thinking he'd dreamed the whole thing."

"You wouldn't be laughing if it'd happened to you," I said.

Helmuth looked thoughtful. "It was close,

but we've got too much left to do to stop now."

"Is that all you're worried about? Handing out your little leaflets?" My stomach was churning. "What about me? I could be rotting in Gestapo hell."

Helmuth's eyes bored into mine. "We agreed the risk was worth it," he said. "That's why we each pledged to take the blame if one of us is caught."

"But are we making any difference?" I asked. "I'm not sure the risk is worth it."

"I won't back out on you, Helmuth, but I'd hate to die for nothing," Karl added.

Helmuth stood. "But this is our war! It's what God wants us to do, even if we die trying."

"You think God wants us to die?" I asked.

"No, of course not," said Helmuth. "But the scriptures are full of martyrs. We're doing God's work."

Karl sighed. "Okay, but I'm not the martyr type. So let's do God's work. *Carefully.*"

"Amen," I said.

Helmuth reached under his bed and pulled out his latest stack of paper, full sheets covered with typing. The opening paragraph quoted Hitler's book, *Mein Kampf*. In writing about World War I, he'd said, "The English soldier could never feel that he had been misinformed by his own countrymen, as unhappily was so much the case with the German soldier that in the end he rejected everything coming from this source as 'swindles' and 'bunk.'"

"Is the same thing happening in this war?" the flyer asked. "Are we being lied to by the German High Command, while the English tell the truth?" Then, for several paragraphs, Helmuth compared German and British battle statistics, presenting a strong argument that the Nazi reports were lies. The handbill ended with a schedule for the BBC broadcasts.

When Karl finished reading, he stood and applauded.

Helmuth grinned. "I'm only telling the truth, like a good Mormon should."

"It's a work of art," I said.

The longer handbills were much better, but it took Helmuth hours and hours to make enough copies. We each took ten.

"Fold them," said Helmuth. "In half, twice. So they're the same size as our old leaflets."

While we folded the handbills, I wondered if I could dig up the courage to deliver them. Last night was too fresh in my mind. I must have looked grim, because Helmuth suddenly gathered up all the flyers and hid them next to the radio.

"Time for a break," he said. "These will wait until tomorrow. We can still catch a late film if we hurry."

"Amen!" I said again. Karl laughed.

We jumped up to leave, but Helmuth stopped us. He put out his hand, palm down, and held it there until we got the idea. I edged my hand over his; Karl placed his on top of mine.

"Let's renew our pledge," Helmuth said.

Chapter Eleven

One evening in early October, Helmuth and Karl appeared at my apartment door, wearing their homburg hats and scarves.

"Get dressed," Helmuth said. "And hurry."

"What is it?" I asked without much enthusiasm. I'd just started a new job, apprenticing with the North German Coal and Coke Works as a machinist, and my first week had been a nightmare. I was tired and depressed and didn't feel like fighting Nazis that night.

"It's Brother Salomon Schwarz," Karl answered. "Things have been happening to him."

"He was sent to a concentration camp," said Helmuth. "They nearly killed him."

Salomon had a Jewish mother, but he'd joined our church.

A shiver went through me, and I hurried toward my room to dress.

"What's this?" Mutti stepped from the kitchen, stopping me. "What's happened to Brother Schwarz?"

Helmuth jumped at the sound of my mother's voice, but he recovered quickly. "He's been away, Sister Ollenik," he answered smoothly. "But he's back, so we wanted to visit."

"Helmuth, I'm not so old that my hearing is bad. You said concentration camp. And I'm not senile, either. Ever since President Zander posted his NO JEWS sign, I knew bad things were going to happen to poor Salomon. Now tell me the truth."

Helmuth looked at the floor.

Mutti smiled grimly. "I'm not going to stop you. Just tell me what happened."

"Salomon applied to the Racial Control Office for an exemption when Jews were forced to wear yellow stars," said Helmuth. "But the office in Hamburg wouldn't give him an answer, so he went to Berlin. While there, he was arrested for not wearing the star. He barely survived the camp."

"Did the RCO ever make a decision?" she asked.

Helmuth's eyes flashed. "They said that only a Jew would touch a Jewish woman, so that proved that Salomon was a full-blooded Jew."

"Brilliant Nazi logic," Mutti said. "At least he's home again."

"Not for long," said Karl. "He's being moved to the Jewish ghetto. This may be our last chance to see him."

Mutti's face sagged. "God help him," she murmured.

"We'd better go, Mutti," I said.

She hugged each of us. "You're good boys. Be careful."

I quickly dressed to look older, and then we hurried away from the apartment. We had a long trolley ride to Barmbek, where Salomon was staying with his grandparents.

Blackout bulbs inside the car made the trip seem even longer. Eerie blue light bathed our faces with a deathly pallor, and no one spoke above a whisper. We looked and sounded like a trolley of corpses, bound straight for the underworld. It was a relief to step from the streetcar into the solid black of night.

Salomon's grandmother, Frau Schwarz, met us at the door. Her shoulders drooped, and she looked worn out. Though they weren't Jews, the Schwarzes were still in danger for boarding their part-Jewish grandson. They were not Mormons, either, but seemed to understand his deep religious convictions.

As we entered the room, Salomon raised his hand in greeting. He seemed too weak to stand, and it was plain that he'd been badly beaten and starved.

"How is the choir doing?" he asked.

"We can barely carry a tune without you," said Helmuth.

Salomon smiled. "How I miss singing with you. Maybe I'll start a choir in the ghetto."

"Where will you stay?" Helmuth asked.

"My sister Anna and my mother are already there. I'll be with them. I'd be there now, but my grandparents were able to hold on to me until I recover." Salomon paused. "I have a new name, you know."

"I know," Helmuth said softly.

"Israel." He spat out the word. "My new middle name, exactly the same as every other Jewish man. We are all Israel now." He shook his head, tears marking his cheeks. "The Nazis have given it a new definition—dog, rat . . . pig. But Israel means one who prevails with God."

We stayed until his eyes grew heavy. Then we each hugged him in turn, pressing our extra money into his hands.

We never saw him again.

Helmuth would have made a great spy. Somehow, he was able to convince President Zander that he'd come to believe in the Nazis. His acting skill paid off—eventually, Zander gave Helmuth a key to his office so that he could come in anytime to do his clerking. That meant he had easier access to paper and to the duplicating machine.

From mid-September on, Helmuth had been producing full-page handbills with detailed information from the BBC broadcasts. He had one new flyer for us each week. This required much more paper, and he began "borrowing" from Social Services. "Finally putting Hitler's paper to some good use," he would say.

Even with "donations" from Social Services and the church, it was never enough. We chipped in what little money we had to buy more paper and supplies. Even then, Helmuth complained about how few handbills he was able to make.

I thought there were plenty of handbills. I was finding it hard to distribute my share because I had to walk farther and farther from my street to find new places. Until I could get rid of them, I stashed the extras in my secret hiding place—a deep hole in my bedroom wall behind a loose piece of wallpaper. I'd hung a tapestry that once belonged to my grandmother over the spot and then used the hole like a safe to hide my private things.

As it turned out, Helmuth couldn't get the duplicating machine to produce good, clear copies. The bluish letters were just too faded. So he continued typing the leaflets using carbon paper. I was relieved because I was sure that Zander would catch us using the duplicator. But my relief didn't last long—Helmuth soon came up with an even riskier idea.

"I've been feeling out others who might help us," Helmuth said casually during one of our meetings in his room.

I was lazily taking in the smells of Frau

Sudrow's Christmas baking, barely paying attention, until Karl jumped to his feet.

"*What?*" Karl stared at Helmuth in disbelief. "Are you crazy? It's too dangerous. What's wrong with you? You should have asked us first."

"We—We don't need anyone else," I stammered.

"Just think what we could do with the right people," Helmuth said. "For instance, someone who'd let us use a printing press."

"Who else knows about us?" asked Karl.

"Only one other person. His name is Gerhard Bauer, and he works with me at Social Services. He hates the Nazis as much as we do. He's even distributed a few of our handbills."

"I can't believe you didn't tell us," I said.

"And what about this printing press?" Karl paced the room furiously. "That should be really easy to keep secret."

"Calm down," said Helmuth. "The fellows at the print shop don't know anything. Not yet, anyway. But Gerhard's known them for years and says they're trustworthy. Still, I haven't given him the green light."

Karl picked up his coat and started for the door. "Count me out," he said.

"Wait!" Helmuth grabbed Karl's sleeve.

Karl shook off his hand.

"This job is too big for three of us," Helmuth said. "I can't type enough handbills. And even if I could, then we'd have trouble distributing them. We need paper, typewriter ribbons, everything. We have to have help."

"But you don't have to sign up people behind our backs," Karl said, his voice like ice.

"Gerhard is right for us. I'm sure. But I should have told you about him first. I'm sorry. But we do need his help."

"That's big of you," said Karl.

Helmuth sighed. "I'll let you know before I do anything else. We'll decide together. Agreed?"

"First I want to meet Gerhard," Karl said. "Then I'll decide what to do."

"Okay," said Helmuth. "But Gerhard thinks he can get someone to translate the handbills into French. Then we could send them to the western front or sneak them in to French prisoners of war."

"How could you make all these plans without us?" I asked. "How could you do that to us?"

"Look, Gerhard doesn't know about the two of you, either," said Helmuth. "That way if something went wrong, you'd be safe."

"Aren't you noble," said Karl. "So why are you telling us about him now?"

"Three reasons. First, I wanted to be certain my feelings about Gerhard were right, and now I'm absolutely sure. Second, using the printing press is a big operation. We'd all have to be on the same page to make it work. Third, I was feeling bad about not telling you."

Karl closed his eyes. "Don't do anything like that again," he said. "It's too risky."

Helmuth smiled. "By the way, I took back all the banned books."

"Good," said Karl. "That's one less risk."

There was a tap at the door, and Frau Sudrow stuck her head in the room. "Helmuth, your mother is here." Her face puckered. "Your stepfather, too. He wants to see you."

Helmuth paled, his mouth a narrow line. Without a word, he stood and followed his grandmother. Karl and I looked at each other, then trailed behind.

"My boy!" Emma Hübener rushed forward to hug Helmuth.

Helmuth returned his mother's hug. He looked coldly at his stepfather, who briefly placed his hand on Helmuth's shoulder.

"We're on our way to the opera," Emma said. "Hugo wanted to stop and say hello." She held Helmuth's face in her hands. "Seeing you on Sundays isn't enough, Liebchen. Why don't you come over more often?"

"We'd like that," said Corporal Hübener.

I was surprised once again by his pleasant face and gentle voice, which contrasted sharply with his dark SS uniform.

"It's true, we don't see much of you," Hugo continued. "And your Hitler Jugend platoon doesn't either, from what I hear."

"I've had a full schedule. With my new apprenticeship," Helmuth answered quietly. "My dues are paid up."

"He's a good boy, Hugo," said Frau Sudrow. "And he has been busy with his work."

Corporal Hübener smiled. "Your leaders asked me to check on you, and I said I would.

Try a little harder, Helmuth. It's best for everyone."

Helmuth shrugged.

Hugo Hübener crossed his arms and studied Helmuth for a moment. "I'll tell them how demanding your work is," he said finally. "After all, you are apprenticing with a government office. That should count for something. Still, you should do your duty whenever possible."

When Helmuth didn't answer, Corporal Hübener turned to me. "Nice to see you again, Rudi. Who's your friend?"

"Oh, that's right," said Emma. "You've never met Karl. This is another of Helmuth's friends, Karl Schneider."

Hugo shook Karl's hand. Despite his friendliness, the air was thick with tension. I couldn't keep my eyes from the red swastika armband. It was so very red against the black uniform.

"Well, we must be off," Emma said a little too brightly. She kissed Helmuth's cheek.

Hugo helped Emma with her coat, then turned back to Helmuth. "Come by soon," he said.

He looked at the rest of us and raised his hand chest high. "Heil Hitler," he said. Herr

Sudrow, who seemed to be dozing in his chair, stiffened.

Karl and I barely moved our arms in weak salutes, and neither of us said anything. Hugo looked at us for longer than I liked, then he nodded and took his wife's arm. "We must be going. Can't be late for the Führer's favorite opera, can we?"

Corporal Hübener swung open the door to find a tall young fellow knocking on empty air.

"Gerhard," said Helmuth. "How nice to see you."

Chapter Twelve

"Who was the SS corporal?" Gerhard asked the moment we were back in Helmuth's room. "I nearly pissed my pants when the door opened. And who are these people? We had private business to take care of tonight."

"He's my stepfather," Helmuth said.

Gerhard's eyes bulged.

"Meet Karl Schneider and Rudi Ollenik— the real reason I asked you over. We've known one another since we were in diapers. They're Mormons, too."

"*This* is the private business? Meeting your church friends?" asked Gerhard.

"Karl and Rudi have been listening to the BBC with me. They've passed out handbills since the beginning. You didn't know about them; they didn't know about you. It's time to come together."

I watched Gerhard's face closely. I expected shock, fear, anger. Instead, he laughed.

"I guess this means we all passed your test," Gerhard said. "We're in the club, boys. Now we're one big happy Hitler-ass-kicking family."

"Gerhard has such a way with words," said Helmuth.

"You're not mad?" I asked.

Gerhard shook his head. "Helmuth's the captain of this ship. It doesn't surprise me that he had you fellows on board. Anyone else we don't know about?"

Karl scowled. "Good question."

"And one I've already answered, Karl. But for Gerhard's ears, I'll say it once more—no, there's no one else to worry about."

"What about your stepfather?" Gerhard asked. "I'd say he's a worry."

"I hardly ever see him. . . ." Helmuth paused. "Wait a minute. I've been so busy hating the fine corporal that I missed the obvious: he's good cover."

Gerhard looked puzzled, then nodded. "I see what you mean."

"I don't," I said.

"I'm the stepson of an SS corporal," said Helmuth. "I can hide in his shadow—the Nazis will give me some leeway. Isn't he going to take care of my HJ leaders?"

"Not if you keep snubbing him," said Karl.

"No problem. If I can play along with Zander, I can be polite to Hübener. But only when I see him, which won't be often."

"Congratulations, Helmuth. You're a hell of a sneak," said Gerhard. "That's something to be proud of."

"Thanks," said Helmuth, grinning. "I work hard at it."

Gerhard grabbed my hand, shaking it vigorously. "You're Rudi, right?"

I nodded and couldn't help smiling.

"And you're Karl."

Instead of taking Gerhard's hand, Karl stepped back. "Hi," he said, his face stony.

Gerhard shrugged and turned to Helmuth. "So, your stepfather's taking care of your HJ leaders. What's that about?"

"Helmuth hasn't been attending his meetings," said Karl. "None of us goes very often."

"It might be smart if you did," said Gerhard.

I shook my head. "Jungvolk was bad enough."

"Gerhard's right," said Helmuth. "About me, at least."

"But it's what we're fighting against," I said.

"We're not fighting out in the open, Rudi. To survive, we have to stay hidden. That's why I put on an act for Zander."

"Don't you think Zander might be suspicious? After all, you did change overnight," said Karl. "I think Corporal Hübener is going to wonder, too."

"Maybe," said Helmuth. "But I don't think so. Every week Zander pats me on the back and tells me how smart I've gotten. Making a few more HJ meetings might do the same thing for my leaders."

Karl snorted in disgust.

"It's fun, in a way," said Gerhard. "I make a private joke out of everything, pretending to believe all that garbage they dish out. And when we shout the Nazi greeting together, I say 'Up yours' instead of 'Heil Hitler.'"

For the first time, Karl smiled. "It may make sense," he said, "but I don't think I can do it. Going once a month is about all I can stand."

"You wouldn't have to go much more than that," said Gerhard.

"Maybe we'd look more suspicious by becoming regulars," I said. "They might think we're coming just to look innocent."

"No chance of that," said Helmuth. "Like President Zander, they'll think we've seen the light. The prodigal sons returned."

"I won't do it," I said. "I hate HJ."

"Rudi's right on this one," said Karl.

"No one's forcing you. But with Hugo on the alert, I'd be smart to show my face every week or two," said Helmuth. He reached behind the Rola and came out with a new stack of handbills. "Funny Corporal Hübener should bother me about the HJ tonight. Take a look."

The handbill was titled "Hitler Jugend." It wasn't Helmuth's longest flyer, but the words almost filled the page.

HITLER JUGEND

German youths, are you actually aware of what the Hitler Jugend is and what goals it pursues? You cannot know it. Your high-handed leaders and subleaders always preach about comradeship, while they exclude themselves from the circle of comradeship. They feel just fine in their element when they can tyrannize the intimidated youths, when they can tyrannize you. Or do you perhaps want to dispute that they want to make you submissive with all the means available? They threaten you with disciplinary punishments, police measures, and have your freedoms taken away from you, from you Germans, and stick you in so-called weekend detention.

So this is the Hitler Jugend, praised far and wide. A compulsory organization of the first order for the recruiting of Nazi-enslaved national comrades. Hitler and his accomplices know that they must deprive

you of your free will at the beginning, in order to make submissive,
spineless creatures out of you. For
Hitler knows that his contemporaries
are beginning gradually to see through
him, the suppressor of free nations,
the murderer of millions.

Therefore we are calling out to
you: Do not let your free will, the
most valuable thing you possess, be
taken away. Do not let yourselves be
suppressed and tyrannized by your
leaders—high-handed kings in minia-
ture—but rather turn your back on
the Hitler Jugend, the tool of the
Hitler regime for your destruction.

We are with you and you can always count on our help!

"Endure to the end, Germany awake!"

<u>This is a chain letter, so pass
it on!</u>

"This is one of your best, Helmuth," said
Gerhard.

"It's a great flyer," Karl agreed. "So good
that I'm going to take its advice." He looked up

at Helmuth. "My back is turned, and it's going to stay that way."

"Amen," I said.

Helmuth smiled. "Nailed to the wall by my own words."

"But you'd be playing a game," said Gerhard. "Laughing at them the whole time. That counts as turning your back, doesn't it?"

"Just being with Nazis gives them power over you. That's what I meant when I wrote this. I can't tell other fellows to stay away if I'm not willing to."

"But they don't have the SS breathing down their necks."

"Shut up, Gerhard." Karl's voice was low and hard. "Helmuth's the captain, remember. He can make up his own mind."

"Okay, okay. Calm down." Gerhard backed over to the bed and sat down.

"On with business," said Helmuth. "What about the press?"

Gerhard's face brightened. "They'll do it," he said. "It was your last flyer that sold them."

"You showed them a flyer?" Karl reached Gerhard in two gigantic strides, grabbing his shirt and lifting him from the bed.

"They're my cousins!" Gerhard cried. "They printed the Jewish Hitler posters!"

Karl dropped him and stepped back. We all knew the posters he meant. They showed Hitler with the big nose Nazis always put on drawings of Jews. He also had a Star of David on his armband instead of a swastika. The Gestapo were trying to crush a rumor that Hitler's father was the illegitimate son of a rich Austrian Jew, and so this drawing drove them wild. If Gerhard's cousins had printed those pictures, which ended up on walls and bulletin boards around Hamburg, then they were crazier than we were.

"I don't like you making decisions for the rest of us," Karl said.

"There was no risk. None," said Gerhard. "My cousins hate Hitler worse than you do. Even so, I wouldn't tell them Helmuth's name."

Karl's laugh was scornful. "The Gestapo will wring your name out of your cousins. Then Helmuth's name out of you."

"That's enough, Karl," said Helmuth. "What's done is done. But you're right about making decisions. We'll do it together from now on. Understand, Gerhard?"

"Sure, whatever Karl says."

Helmuth put a hand on Karl's arm to hold him back, then took a deep breath. "Should we go ahead with the printing press?" he asked.

"If Gerhard is the only contact," said Karl. "I don't want his cousins finding out your name or ours."

"Fine with me," said Gerhard. "They can't start for a while, anyhow, because they need to save out paper and ink with every job so the boss won't miss any supplies. But they'll get to it in a few weeks."

Helmuth noticed I was fidgeting. "Rudi?"

"The whole idea scares me."

"And it should," said Karl. "Rudi and I have put up with your surprises, Helmuth, but don't think we're pushovers. From now on, we vote on everything."

"Then what about finding someone to translate the handbills into French?" Gerhard asked.

"Why bother? Most of the French hate Hitler," I said.

"The world thinks all Germans worship Hitler," said Helmuth. "I want them to know we don't. So let's start with France."

"And just how are we going to do that?" I asked.

"We'll find the right people," said Helmuth, and I had the feeling he already knew who they were.

"And who's going to translate?" asked Karl. "Let me guess. . . . Gerhard has another cousin who speaks French."

Gerhard smiled. "No, just a good friend."

"Too much, too fast," Karl said.

"Karl's right," said Helmuth. "Let's worry about the printing press for now. We'll come back to the translations later."

Helmuth leaned over to turn on the radio. "It's almost ten o'clock. We nearly missed the BBC."

I hardly heard the broadcast. Finding out about Gerhard and the printing press jumbled my thinking, causing my mind to wander. While the words washed over me, I thought for the first time about being a traitor. Until now, though I'd been scared, I'd treated all this as a dangerous game. But that night I faced up to the complete truth. We were traitors—enemies of the state—and I imagined myself in front of a firing squad.

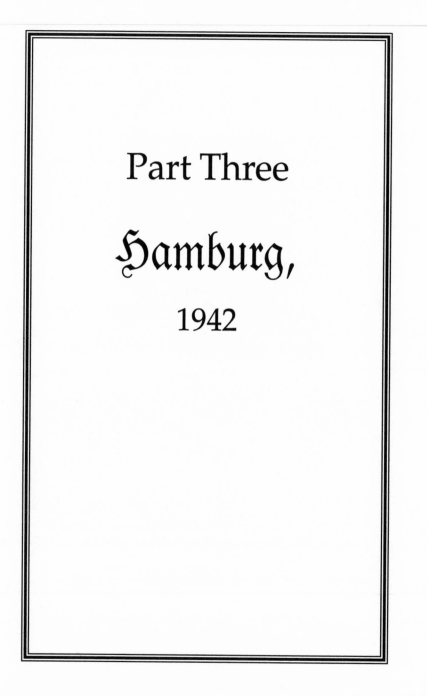

Part Three

Hamburg,

1942

Chapter Thirteen

Yet another Christmas season came and passed, only now Hitler's armies were beginning to stumble. But the worst news for Germany had come a few weeks before Christmas—Japan's surprise bombing of Pearl Harbor. When the Americans joined the war, they were also fighting against Japan's ally—us.

On New Year's Eve, I was back on air-raid watch with Helmuth and Karl. This time we were alone, without an adult. At first we thought it would be fun, but it didn't turn out that way—instead, a terrible emptiness filled us as we remembered last year's watch with Brother Worbs. So rather than listen to music, we bundled up and spent most of our time on the roof.

"Do you think American planes will bomb us?" I asked while staring into the night sky.

"Yes," said Helmuth. "Not tonight, but yes."

"Just think, men from Utah might be in those bombers. We could be killed by fellow Mormons." Karl shook his head.

In early January, Helmuth wrote his longest handbill.

> Comrades in the north, south, east, west. Friends at home! A new year has begun, a year upon which Hitler has set all of his last hopes in this struggle, which is in fact already hopelessly lost.

Helmuth then carefully tore apart the recent Nazi reports about the war, including "facts" about North Africa and the Russian front. "Germans, arise, make your decision," he concluded. "A determined deed can still rescue you and your country from the abyss to which Hitler has led you with his sweet talk. Make your decision before it is too late!"

* * *

"Have you heard people talking?" asked Gerhard. We were all in Helmuth's room for the BBC report. "Our flyers are driving the Gestapo crazy! The pigs are tearing up Hamburg trying to find us."

"I don't like this," I said. "Maybe we should lie low—"

"No!" Helmuth shook his head. "Not now—not when we're finally having an effect. Now's the time to fan the fire. And here's why." He tossed me a Nazi pamphlet, *The Bible, Not God's Word,* by General Erich Ludendorff.

"This is a holy war—our holy war," Helmuth said. "And this is our answer to Hitler." He pulled out a handful of flyers and gave each of us a copy.

His new handbill started by quoting Ludendorff's pamphlet: "The Bible not God's word. Merely a scheme of the Jewish world to enslave mankind. The product of an overactive imagination."

"So now they're going after Christian churches, too?" I asked. "How can that help them?"

"Adolf thinks he's God," Karl said.

"Read," Helmuth ordered.

" 'Christians, arise,' " I read out loud. " 'Open the Bible, read what it says in the Book of the Prophet Daniel, 11:21: And in his estate shall stand up a vile person, to whom they shall not give the honor of the kingdom: but he shall come in peaceably, and obtain the kingdom by flatteries.

" 'To whom does this apply better than to the Führer who won over Germany with his bold speeches and grandiose promises?' " the flyer asked.

"Daniel was talking about modern days," Helmuth said. "Maybe he actually foresaw Hitler."

"I like the idea of using religion as a weapon against the Nazis," said Gerhard. "Let's hope the churches join us. Too bad we couldn't use the printing press for this one."

"What about the press?" Karl asked. "It's been weeks and nothing's happened. Are your cousins backing out?"

"You'd like that, wouldn't you?" said Gerhard. "But it took a while to save enough ink and paper. They're nearly ready."

"Good—it's about time." Helmuth smiled.

"I'm burning up typewriter ribbons faster than Hitler can burn up books."

"Maybe it's time to translate the handbills," I said. I couldn't believe the suggestion came from me.

Karl stared at me, then looked at Helmuth. "Let's do it."

Gerhard let out a whoop. "I'm mixed up in a Mormon crusade! 'Onward, Christian soldiers—'"

"Shut up," said Karl, his voice dangerous.

Gerhard shifted uncomfortably. "Sorry," he mumbled.

"We're all agreed, then," said Helmuth. "Gerhard and I will talk to the guy we mentioned before. The one who speaks French. He works with us at Social Services."

Before the end of January, they finally approached Gerhard's friend, Werner Kranz.

On the first Sunday in February, Helmuth pulled Karl and me aside at church to tell us about Werner.

"He won't do it," Helmuth said.

"Why not?" I asked. "Gerhard seemed so sure about him."

Helmuth shrugged. "He was scared."

"That's great," said Karl. "Just great. He'll probably run right to the Gestapo."

"No. Werner hates the Nazis," Helmuth said.

Karl snorted. "Or so he says. What do we know about him? Nothing."

"Gerhard knew something," I said. "We had to trust him."

"No, we didn't!" Karl slapped his hand against the wall. "We could have met Werner first. Felt him out. Now . . ."

"Now we'll find somebody else to translate." Helmuth's voice was firm. "That's all this means, Karl. Werner won't turn us in."

"He's a coward," said Karl. "He'll fold the first time a Gestapo agent looks at him funny."

"Anything's possible," Helmuth said quietly. "It's part of the risk. We can't do this without risk."

"Talk to him again," I said. "Invite him over to listen to the BBC. Maybe he'll change his mind."

"What do you think, Karl?" Helmuth asked.

Karl stared into space, his face unreadable. Finally, he answered. "He already knows about us. What other choice do we have?"

Helmuth nodded. "I'll get him over here."

But the next week was a busy one for all of us. We didn't have a chance to get together, and on Sunday morning, Helmuth didn't show up at church.

Karl laughed nervously. "Maybe he had a hot date last night."

"Something went wrong," I said.

"Stop it!" he whispered. "Don't be so jumpy."

"Then where are the Sudrows?" I asked.

Neither Helmuth nor his grandparents came that evening, either.

After sacrament meeting, President Zander asked everyone to remain seated for a moment. "I have alarming news that must be shared with all of you." He paused ominously. "Helmuth Guddat has been arrested by the Gestapo."

Suddenly it seemed as if there was no air left to breathe.

"I don't know the details," President Zander continued. "Only that he was arrested for traitorous activities."

Zander's face suddenly hardened and so did his voice. His eyes wandered toward Karl and me. "Brother Guddat violated the trust of this branch. As you know, he was my clerk and was using the church typewriter to write letters to our servicemen. He misused that trust to produce antigovernment propaganda. Now we have no typewriter. The Gestapo confiscated it as evidence."

His eyes roved the room, stopping again on the two of us. "He has endangered each member of our branch. We are all tainted now in the eyes of the Gestapo. So be careful how you act, for the sake of your brothers and sisters. For the sake of our church's existence in Germany."

If President Zander said more, I didn't hear it. Blood pounded in my ears, and I felt faint. Karl led me outside, where the winter air brought me back to my senses. The first thing I noticed was the wild look in Karl's eyes. He was as scared as I was.

We were both thinking the same thing. Would Helmuth be true to our pledge? *Could* Helmuth be true to our pledge? We'd made our promises to one another so easily. But now our bold words seemed childish. Even if Helmuth kept quiet, the Gestapo would be on our doorsteps anyway because the three of us were best friends.

The noose tightened around us.

Three days later, I turned sixteen. Karl and I had decided to lie low, so he didn't even come to the party my mother gave for me.

I couldn't sleep at nights, waiting for loud banging on our door, waiting for the Gestapo. Mutti noticed, and she asked me again and again, "Did you know what Helmuth was up to?"

"No," I answered. It hurt to lie, but what else could I do? Telling her the truth would put her in danger.

Not knowing what had happened to Helmuth only made things worse. How did he get caught? Who had given him away? Even the newspapers had little to say, except that Gerhard had been arrested, too.

Finally, I took a risk and visited Helmuth's grandparents. Since the Gestapo would probably be watching their apartment, I asked my mother to bake a raisin cake to take as a gift. I hoped the Gestapo would see me only as an errand boy.

Frau Sudrow's eyes were red and swollen, and Herr Sudrow sat rigidly in his chair, staring vacantly. When I saw them, I was more frightened than ever. Frau Sudrow pulled me inside and sat beside me on the sofa, taking my hands in her wrinkled grasp.

"Did you help Helmuth do these things?" she asked, her dark eyes boring into mine.

When I didn't answer, Frau Sudrow nodded. "Foolish," she murmured.

Herr Sudrow grunted in agreement.

"How did they find him out?" I whispered. "I need to know."

Frau Sudrow lowered her voice, too. "They told me nothing. But I listened when they brought him here to search his room."

Her voice broke. "They had beaten him. His face . . ." Tears tumbled down her cheeks. We sat quietly for a while until Frau Sudrow was able to swallow back her sobbing.

"They found a shortwave radio," she finally managed to say. "And a typewriter. It was hidden in Helmuth's trunk and still had an unfinished page in the carriage. Of course, they confiscated everything." She shook her head sadly. "What a foolish old woman I am, never to have noticed what was happening."

"It was better you didn't know," I said.

Herr Sudrow cleared his throat. "We might have stopped him," he said, without looking at us. "And you. If we had known. We are as much to blame."

I wanted to say something comforting. To assure him that none of this was their fault. But I sat instead in silent misery. It all seemed unreal, a nightmare from which I would suddenly, thankfully awaken.

Frau Sudrow's quiet voice broke the silence. "An overseer from work heard Helmuth and Gerhard talking to another boy about the handbills. They were in a storage room and didn't know the overseer used the place for his noon-hour naps. He'd hidden himself behind some boxes. The Gestapo agents laughed and said, 'It's a good thing Herr Mohns can hear in his sleep.'" Her eyes filled with tears again. "Then they hit Helmuth so hard he fell to the floor."

Helmuth hadn't been careful enough. He should never have talked to Werner anywhere in the Social Services building. They should have gone outside at lunch break. Or met after work. But then, who would have guessed someone was sleeping in the storage room?

"One more thing," said Frau Sudrow. "The Gestapo agents told Helmuth that everyone had abandoned him. 'Even Gerhard has turned on you—he brought Herr Mohns one of your flyers,' they said."

"I don't think you can trust what the Gestapo says, Sister Sudrow. Gerhard wouldn't do that. He wouldn't."

But I wasn't so sure.

Chapter Fourteen

The next day was Sunday. I hadn't seen Karl for a week and wanted to tell him what I'd learned from Frau Sudrow. But when I reached the church, Karl's sister was waiting for me. She pulled me outside, her face frantic.

"The Gestapo arrested Karl yesterday!" she cried. "They're coming after you next, Rudi!"

My heart stopped beating. "Go back inside, Karla."

She didn't move. "What will you do, Rudi?"

"I don't know. Now go inside. You don't want to be seen talking to me." I nudged Karla toward the door, my hands shaking. "Thanks for warning me," I whispered.

She smiled weakly, her lips trembling, and disappeared inside the church. I turned and ran.

I raced home and hid in my room like a frightened child. I thought about trying to run away, escaping to Sweden or Switzerland. But it would be hard to get out of Germany. And even if I could, the Gestapo would punish my mother instead of me. That's what they did.

When my mother came home from church she'd put two and two together. She slammed into our apartment, calling out in a loud, frenzied voice.

"Rudi! Rudi, are you here?"

She opened my door and spotted me sitting on the floor between my bed and the wall. "Rudi, you've heard about Karl. What have you done? Oh, Rudi, baby, what have you done? What have you done?"

"What I thought was right, Mutti," I answered, my voice cracking. "I'm sorry I lied."

"You promised me you'd be careful!" she cried. "Was this being careful?"

I shook my head.

"You know how I feel about the Nazis. And how your father felt. But we can't beat them. We have to wait them out."

"I don't think we can outlast them," I said.

"Can we sit and wait for someone like Hitler to just go away?"

"You're only boys," she said. "You're still children! Did you think you could take on Hitler? This is Helmuth's fault. Look where acting so smart got him—and you!"

"No, Mutti, don't blame Helmuth. We all agreed. We made a pledge."

Mutti stared at me from the doorway.

"I'm sorry I lied to you, but I didn't want them hurting you because of me."

"The Gestapo will take you away!" my mother screamed. "Oh, dear God, what can we do?"

She rushed to where I was huddled, kneeling and putting her arms around me. We stayed there, clutching each other, until evening's shadows crept into the room.

I didn't leave the apartment Monday morning, as if staying inside would protect me from the Gestapo. But there proved to be some comfort in following my usual routine again. Tuesday passed as a normal day, and I began to breathe easier. But with my new sense of relief came terrible pangs of guilt. My friends were gone—

probably being tortured by the Gestapo. Yet somehow they'd managed to keep me safe. Instead of worrying about them, I had been worrying only about myself. One minute I'd feel euphoric that I was free; the next would bring unbearable grief.

Wednesday morning I felt almost light-hearted with relief as I sat in my technical drafting class. Then there was a knock on the classroom door, and the school principal appeared.

"Ollenik," he said curtly. "Come with me."

I don't remember walking to his office. But I do remember the door swinging open to reveal two men wearing long black leather coats and wide-brimmed hats. The taller man flipped his lapel to reveal a badge. "Gestapo! Inspector Wangemann, and this is Officer Müssener. Our car is waiting."

My books stayed on my desk, my coat in the cloakroom. I never saw them again.

The black Mercedes-Benz sped toward Rothenburgsort and my mother's apartment. My mind was a blank, but I do remember wondering which shift Mutti was working and praying that she wasn't home.

The car finally pulled up in front of our place. Müssener and Wangemann hustled me up the stairs and banged on our apartment door. When no one answered, they banged again, and I knew my silent prayer had been answered.

"Do you have your key?" Müssener asked.

I nodded dumbly. I fumbled with the lock. The second it clicked, Wangemann shoved the door open and pushed me into the apartment.

"Take us to your room," said Müssener.

The numbness was beginning to wear off. I started to shake as I led them to my bedroom door. Wangemann noticed.

"Shaking in your boots, Ollenik?" He smiled. It was a smile that harbored no kindness. "You ought to be. In fact, you ought to be so scared you're pissing your pants." He shoved me into my room and banged me against the wall. "Stand right there and don't move," he said.

"You can save us and yourself some trouble," said Müssener, his voice gentle. "It will go easier for you if you tell us where they are."

"What are you looking for?" I asked.

Wangemann slapped me so hard my head bounced off the wall. I cried out, and he hit me again. "We don't have time for games," he shouted, his nose nearly touching mine. "We know about you. Your friends have given you away. They told us about the handbills you hide in your room."

Tears welled in my eyes, and Wangemann hit me again. Then Müssener stepped between us, carefully pushing Wangemann away. "Just tell us where to look," he said calmly. "It is too late for pretending, Rudi. Helmuth told us you had them. And so did Karl."

I shook my head, and Müssener stepped aside. Wangemann was on me in a second, slapping and punching.

"I don't have any!" I cried.

He hit me one more time, knocking me into a corner of the room. I stood there, shivering with pain and praying there weren't any handbills in my "safe." I'd checked a dozen times in the past three days, but Wangemann made me doubt my own probing fingers. What if one had slipped to the side or been wedged in a crevice? Suddenly, the tapestry covering the hole in my wall was like a magnet pulling my eyes. I forced myself to look away from it.

"I believe you," Müssener said. "But we must search. To satisfy our superiors, you understand."

Müssener looked behind the large gilt-edged mirror over the bureau and behind the few pictures hanging on the wall, while Wangemann attacked the rest of my room. He raked books from shelves and ripped out bureau drawers, smashing them against the wall. He flung clothes from the wardrobe, taking care to rip the linings from suits and coats. When I cried out in protest, he threw a Book of Mormon at my face, bloodying my mouth.

Then Wangemann's eyes fell on the tapestry. I could barely breathe as he walked over and grabbed the edge. He shook it hard, but the nails held. Suddenly he seemed to lose interest in pulling it down; he laughed and pointed to a bugling bull elk that was woven into the fabric. "You'll be howling like this elk when we're finished with you," he said.

The Gestapo agents hauled me back to the Mercedes. As we drove downtown, I thought about my mother coming home to find my room destroyed. It would be like coming home to find my dead body. What had I done to her? I blinked back the tears.

Hamburg City Hall housed Gestapo head-quarters. The Mercedes pulled up to a special entrance at the rear of the building. The agents dragged me through the back door and into an old elevator that groaned and shuttered as if it, too, were about to be interrogated by Müssener and Wangemann. The lift had only one stop, the cellar. SS guards stood at the elevator doors and at the stairwell.

Müssener guided me down a hall and into a small room with only a table and four chairs. The chairs sat against the wall, but he pointed to the center of the room. "Please, Rudi, stand there," he said as he removed his leather over-coat and hat and hung them on wall hooks.

Wangemann did the same while a young blond woman came through the door and pulled a chair over to the table. She sat down and opened a stenographer's pad, ready to take notes.

Wangemann smiled at her and reached into the pocket of his coat. He pulled out a box with a French label. Fine, perfumed soap. Most Ger-mans hadn't washed with decent soap for ages. He pressed the box into her hands and kissed her on the forehead.

Müssener began to speak in a calm voice.

"Please state your name."

"Rudolf Ollenik."

"Where do you live?"

Why was he asking what they already knew? I told him my address, my mother's and father's names, the place I worked, the school I attended. Then Wangemann came to stand on my left and started flinging questions at me.

"State the full name of the Party," he yelled in my ear.

I hesitated, puzzled by such a stupid question. As if anyone in Germany wouldn't know what "Nazi" meant. Then I saw Wangemann raise his gloved hand. "Nationalsozialistische Deutsche Arbeiterpartei," I answered quickly.

"How many points in the Party Program?"

"Twenty-five." Every schoolchild knew these answers.

"The Führer's birth date? Look at me when you answer!" he screamed.

"April 20," I said, forcing myself to meet his eyes.

"The year?"

"1889."

"Who is Hamburg's district leader?

"Karl Kaufmann."

For a moment, I let myself believe that my right answers would appease them.

"When was the last time you listened to the BBC London?" asked Müssener.

I hesitated.

"Eyes up!" Wangemann's tone was deadly.

"How could I listen to the BBC?"

Wangemann's fist connected with my face, sending me to the floor. Lights danced in my head, and there was blood on my tongue. Müssener helped me up. The blond girl busily scribbled in her notebook as if nothing out of the ordinary had happened.

"Now, Rudi, please tell us the truth," Müssener said softly. "We have Helmuth's Rola. We know what you've been up to. No more lies, all right?"

"Did you listen to the BBC in Guddat's apartment?" Wangemann screamed. "Look at me, you traitorous piece of shit!"

Wangemann's face was close to mine. Too

close. My defenses began dropping. Still, I lied to him. "Helmuth had a radio, but we never got it to work. It never picked up the BBC."

I thought he was going to hit me again, but Müssener pushed him away and said, "You had a shortwave radio and never listened to foreign broadcasts? Rudi, Rudi, do you think us stupid?"

"Your mother knew about all of this, didn't she?" Wangeman yelled. "She even helped you deliver the flyers."

"No!" I cried. "No, she didn't even know Helmuth had a shortwave."

"Still, she helped you with the flyers," said Müssener.

"I didn't deliver flyers. I burned them."

"Guddat told us you delivered at least a hundred handbills. Look at me when I speak!" Wangemann slapped the back of my head.

"That's a lie!" I yelled.

Wangemann's boot caught me in the knee. My whole body shook with the pain, and my leg crumpled. I tumbled to the floor, and he continued to kick me. I tried to protect my head, and his boots found my ribs. I was screaming in agony as I looked at Müssener, my eyes begging him to call Wangemann off. It was the last thing I remember.

When I came to, Wangemann and Müssener were gone, and two SS guards were pulling me roughly to my feet. It hurt to open my eyes, and my breath came in short gasps. I held my ribs as the guards pushed me down the hall. A dozen other prisoners formed a line at the bottom of the stairs, and they placed me at the end. Barely able to stand, I was given an identification tag and handcuffed to the man next to me. He didn't even turn my way, but I could see that both his eyes were blackened and his face looked like raw meat.

The guards forced us to stand at silent attention. Somehow, I was able to find the strength to obey their order. One fellow down the line fainted, and the guards kicked him until he pulled himself up again.

Finally, we were led up the stairs and outside to a big green van—the prisoner transport bus. The prisoners called it the Green Tin Can. The van already had a dozen men inside, and I looked to see if Helmuth or Karl or even Gerhard might be on board. I didn't see a familiar face.

"Do you know a prisoner named Helmuth Guddat?" I whispered to the man next to me. "Or Karl Schneider?"

At the sound of my voice, the guard's head snapped in our direction. I shut my mouth and sat in silence, praying for a way out of this mess.

Chapter Fifteen

Concentration camp Fuhlsbüttel. People had whispered about this place—Hamburg's spot for dumping anyone who bothered the Nazis. The Green Tin Can pulled through the gate and stopped in front of the prison.

"*Heraus!*" the guards yelled. "*Schnell!*"

We stood and moved quickly from the bus. My silent companion suddenly leaned near and whispered, "Watch out for Tall Paul."

I didn't have a chance to ask what he meant, but as I was pushed from the bus, I recognized Tall Paul immediately. He stood a head or two above anyone else, with broad shoulders and thick arms to match his height. It was plain to see that this giant reigned over Fuhlsbüttel. He was king of the guards, and his scepter was a long rubber club. All of us were hit or jabbed with it as we passed.

"Move! Move, you filthy pigs!" Tall Paul yelled as he whacked at us. There was a hint of laughter in his voice, and he hit you harder if you slouched or shuffled your feet or looked to the side. I tried hard not to do anything that might draw his attention, but I was already marked.

"Halt!" he called out as I came even with him. "Look at this. They've sent us a baby." He lifted my chin with his club. "How old are you?"

"Sixteen."

The club landed between my shoulder blades, bringing me to my knees and pulling my companion down, too.

"Sixteen, *sir!*" Tall Paul screamed.

"Sixteen, sir," I answered, teeth clenched against the pain.

The giant hoisted me up and glanced at my identification tag. "Why are you here, Ollenik?"

"They say I passed out handbills, sir." My voice was trembling.

"Ah, yes," Tall Paul said calmly. "Your playmates are already here. And I think they may still be alive." Suddenly he exploded. "I know about your handbills! Our Führer is NOT a murderer!" he screamed. The club whipped across my head. "He is NOT a liar!" The club landed on my back. "He is NOT a traitor!" The club connected with my knees.

Each hit burned like fire but wasn't meant to hurt me badly. Maybe Tall Paul was too smart to damage Gestapo property, or maybe he wanted to save me for torturing later. But the blows still had a cumulative effect, and when I thought I couldn't take any more, my handcuffed companion suddenly fainted. He fell hard to the cold paving stones, dragging me down with him. Tall Paul turned his attention to the motionless form, kicking him and cursing.

When kicking didn't bring the man back to his feet, Tall Paul motioned to another guard, who leaned over us and unlocked the handcuffs. Two others grabbed my unwitting rescuer by the arms and dragged him away.

The guards uncuffed the rest of the prisoners and then herded us inside. They pushed me in a different direction because I was new. Then they confiscated what little was in my pockets, as well as my belt and shoelaces, and took me upstairs. We passed through openings in walls made of iron bars and walked by cell after cell. All along the way, the guards would stop and command me to drop to the floor for push-ups or knee bends and kick me if I didn't perform fast enough. Finally we came to a standstill in front of one of the cell doors, and they commanded me to face the wall. I heard the key turning in the lock, and suddenly I was grabbed from behind and shoved through the opening. I fell to the floor as the heavy steel door slammed behind me.

"Stand up, boy."

I yelped and struggled to my feet.

"Quiet, you little fool! Do you want them back in here?"

The voice came from a tall, thin man sitting on one of the two bunks in the cell. He looked to be in his mid-twenties. The man yawned and repositioned the gold wire-rimmed spectacles on his nose.

I glanced at my new surroundings. The bunks were the only furniture, unless you counted a water faucet with a rusty bucket and a toilet.

"Let me tell you how things work," whispered my cellmate. "You'd better listen, or we'll both have hell to pay. Whenever the door opens, you must jump up and stand with your back to the wall. Then you must shout out your name and your crime. For instance, I would shout, 'Protective Custody Prisoner Weber. Arrested for cowardice and for disobeying direct military orders.'"

"Protective Custody Prisoner?" I asked. "What are we being protected from?" I laughed bitterly, and Herr Weber put a finger to his lips.

"You have a lot to learn, boy, if you want to survive. Just do as I say. Jump for the walls every time the door opens."

"But you didn't jump up when they threw me in here."

"I was dozing. The door opened and closed too quickly. But if the guards had entered the cell, I would have been on my feet." Weber lowered his voice even more. "The guards' job is to break us down, make us easier to interrogate. Don't expect to get a good night's sleep. And then it's up at five A.M. to clean this hellhole before a white-glove inspection. The cell will never be clean enough. Never."

I sat on my bunk and noticed Herr Weber was staring at the cell door. I followed his gaze and saw two eyes peering at us through a slot in the steel. We waited silently until the eyes disappeared.

"We are never really alone," Herr Weber whispered. "Come. Wash the blood from your hands and face. It soon will be time to eat."

Instead, I collapsed on the bunk and closed my eyes. This had been the longest day of my life, and all I wanted to do was sleep. But the tinny sound of water striking the bucket roused me.

"Come," Herr Weber repeated. "If you aren't presentable, there will be more hell to pay. And we can't afford bloodstains on the blankets." He came close and leaned over to whisper in my ear. "Who knew the devil was so fastidious? Hell must be a very clean place."

I smiled a little and stood. Every bone and muscle in my body screamed in protest, and I groaned and fell back to the bunk.

"You'll feel worse in the morning. Moving around may keep you from stiffening."

I nodded. Gritting my teeth, I made my way to the bucket. Herr Weber had taken off his shirt, preparing to wash himself, and I caught sight of the underside of his upper arm. I gasped and took a backward step.

He turned his arm and glanced at the tattoo of twin lightning bolts, forming a double *S*. It was the mark of the Waffen-SS, the brutal military arm of Hitler's elite guard. Like the rest of the SS, they were fanatics, but instead of policing Germany, they were sent to fight the Russians and the English.

Herr Weber shrugged and said, "Don't be afraid. I'm considered a traitor. I'm surprised they haven't ripped their sacred emblem from my flesh."

When I still didn't move, he sighed. "I made the rank of first lieutenant in the Waffen-SS because of my father. He is dedicated SS himself and a cruel man. I thought I wanted to be like him." He shook his head as he picked up a sliver of coarse soap and began washing his hands.

"Cruelty is a requirement for the Waffen-SS," he said in a dull voice. "No mercy for enemies of the Reich. Trouble is, everyone is an enemy of the Reich. The Jews. The Poles. The Russians. Even some Germans. Boys like you."

His eyes met mine briefly. "When it came down to it, I couldn't do it. I couldn't be cruel for the Führer. In Russia, I was ordered to shoot a whole family—Jews in a ghetto who were feeding themselves and others by stealing—but I threw down my gun. Because my father is a high-ranking officer, I was sent back to Germany instead of being dealt with there. But to my father, I am dead. To the SS, I soon will be."

"Lieutenant Weber . . . ," I began awkwardly, but I didn't know what to say and fell silent.

"Please, call me Josef."

"I'm Rudi," I said.

Josef handed me the soap and helped me wash away the blood.

Dinner was dry bread crusts, a watery soup of some kind, and imitation coffee. Real coffee was nearly impossible to get these days, and Mormons weren't supposed to drink it anyhow. This brew was made from malt, and it tasted like mud.

I drank it.

Finally, the lights were turned out. Josef had

warned me that sleep was hard to come by in Fuhlsbüttel, but I soon drifted off. It seemed like only seconds when the cell door crashed open and the lights flared.

"Up, up!" Josef yelled.

I hit the wall as Josef called out, "Protective Custody Prisoner Weber! Arrested for cowardice and for disobeying a direct military order!"

"Protective Custody Prisoner Ollenik!" I yelled. "Arrested for allegedly listening to foreign radio broadcasts!"

I saw the guard raise his rubber truncheon, and I turned to the side as he swung at me. His blow missed, but he followed with a vicious kick that caught me in the thigh and sent me sprawling.

"Allegedly?" He laughed. "A young lawyer in the making? Admit the truth, or I'll beat you to death right here. No need for a trial."

I struggled to my feet. "Protective Custody Prisoner Ollenik," I said. "Arrested for listening to foreign broadcasts."

"Haven't you forgotten something?" the guard asked. "Passing out foreign propaganda, that is."

"Protective Custody Prisoner Ollenik," I repeated. "Arrested for listening to foreign broadcasts and distributing foreign news."

As quickly as they'd come, the guards were gone. The cell was dark and quiet. Neither of us spoke.

In a minute or two, Josef's breathing slowed and deepened. But I lay awake for a long time before I finally slept. Then the door banged open and the lights blazed again. We hit the wall. This continued all night—sometimes after thirty minutes, sometimes after two hours. Josef slept between each visit.

I wasn't so lucky.

By morning, I was exhausted. The guards woke us for the final time at 5:00 A.M. When they were gone, Josef announced it was time to clean the cell. We scoured the toilet, wiped the window ledge, and made our beds. The beds had to be as rigid and smooth as a plank—not the tiniest wrinkle.

Soon the guards were back, and the inspection began. One of them ran his finger along the window ledge. Then he looked into the toilet and motioned for Josef to come. Josef slipped off his spectacles and dropped them on the bunk as he walked forward.

Suddenly the SS guard lashed out with his keys, swiping them across Josef's face. Josef fell back, blood gushing from his cheek.

"You call this clean?" the guard screamed. He leaped forward, grabbing Josef by the hair. "We taught you cleanliness in the SS. But you didn't learn. You didn't learn anything about anything!" He kicked the back of Josef's knees, knocking him to the floor, and then crammed his head inside the toilet bowl. "Does that look clean? Does that look clean?" he screamed.

The man straightened, leaving Josef with his face in the toilet. "Take care of it," he said brusquely. Then he and the other guard marched out, slamming the door behind them.

I rushed over to help stop the bleeding.

Josef smiled weakly. "He hasn't used the keys before. He was trying to impress you," he said. "The toilet is never clean enough. Never."

Chapter Sixteen

After a breakfast of dry bread crusts and prison coffee, I was loaded onto the Green Tin Can. The guards took Josef before they came to take me, but I didn't see him on the bus. Maybe he was in one of the solid, cell-like compartments at the rear. Helmuth and Karl didn't seem to be there, either.

We rode in silence to Gestapo headquarters. Guards marched us into a long room, painted glaring white. They called it the Hall of Mirrors. We were lined up right against the wall, our noses touching it. And there we waited. And waited—and waited—standing at attention. We weren't allowed to speak or turn our heads or pee.

I began to wonder if Helmuth or Karl might have been in one of the solitary cells on the bus. I tried to look for them, but something crashed into the wall next to my ear. It was a heavy glass ashtray. The SS guards threw them at anyone who moved.

After two hours of standing, I began drifting in and out of consciousness. Even my fear couldn't keep me awake. Suddenly, I heard footsteps running toward me.

"*Achtung!* Stand straight!"

Barely breathing, I straightened up and stood as rigidly as possible. Then I heard a sharp crack, like a small gun. I leaped back, which earned me a stinging blow that knocked me to the floor.

"Up! Up!" Kicks rained down all over my body—on my neck and shoulders, back and stomach. I struggled to my feet. The prisoner next to me stood with blood streaming down his face. The noise—that loud crack—had been his face slamming into the wall.

"Ollenik! Rudolf Ollenik!" Inspector Wangemann pushed me away from the wall and led me to the same room as yesterday, where Müssener was waiting.

"Hello, Rudi," he said. "Stand where you were before."

There was a faint knock at the door, and the blond stenographer came into the room.

"Marlene!" Wangemann hurried to pull out a chair for her. "I have something for you," he said, pulling a packet from his coat—real Dutch coffee.

Marlene smiled radiantly and took the gift.

"Dinner tonight, Liebling. Remember?" said Wangemann, stroking her cheek.

Marlene nodded. I wondered sourly if she could talk.

"Let's get on with it," said Müssener.

Marlene immediately opened her notebook. Wangemann stopped flirting and looked at me, his eyes narrowing. He picked up a rubber club and placed it under my chin—it was sticky with old blood.

"I'm not in the mood for games today," he whispered. Then he lowered his club to my chest and shoved. Hard. I stumbled backward.

"Stand still!" He whacked me in the stomach, and I peed my pants. I stood there, humiliated, pretending that the stain on my pants didn't exist.

Wangemann lifted my chin with his club. "Guddat gave you twenty handbills a week for months. What did you do with them?"

"He gave me a few. Not that many. I passed them around the neighborhood."

"What neighborhood?"

I was slow to answer, and he slapped me with the back of his gloved hand.

"Where I live!" I cried. "Rothenburgsort."

"Where did you leave them?"

"In mailboxes. On bulletin boards in apartment buildings."

"What streets?

"Kanalstrasse, Marckmannstrasse, Stresowstrasse . . ."

"Good! Now we are getting somewhere. Let's try again. How many handbills did you get from Guddat? And how often?"

I hesitated. How many handbills had been turned over to the Gestapo? Five or ten? Fifteen or twenty? Was I falling into a trap?

He slapped me again, and I decided to take a chance. "He only gave me a few. Two or three times."

"Who listened to the BBC with you in Guddat's apartment? Give me names."

"I wouldn't know. I never listened to it."

Wangemann grabbed my throat, nearly lifting me off the ground. "Liar," he snarled, and hurled me against the wall. Then he marched out of the room.

Müssener watched him go, then pointed to a chair. "Sit down," he said gently. Pulling another chair around, he sat across from me.

"I have sons about your age, Rudi," Müssener said. "This is no fun for me. But it's my job, at least until the war is over."

I looked at him blankly.

"Why, Rudi?" he asked. "Why did you do these things? Hasn't the Fatherland been a good place to live? Are you angry about something?"

"I don't know," I cried, and tears rolled down my cheeks. "It was stupid. Stupid, stupid, stupid!"

"Sometimes our parents make mistakes, too. Doing and saying things they don't mean. Maybe your mother was angry with the Führer and said things that made you angry. I'm afraid all parents do that from time to time."

I shook my head, but I was so worn down I almost told him everything. Instead, I cried like a baby. Müssener let me cry. When I'd dried my eyes, he patted my shoulder, then took me back to the Hall of Mirrors.

Josef was gone when I got back to Fuhlsbüttel. He never returned. Prisoners often disappeared, and it was best to pretend not to notice.

I desperately missed Josef. It was hard to survive a night alone, hitting the wall nearly every hour. Tall Paul made several of the visits, forcing me to do push-ups and knee bends until I was in agony. When my strength gave out, he whacked his club across my shoulders.

The next day I was dragged back to Gestapo headquarters to face Wangemann and Müssener once again.

This time Müssener came to get me as soon as the Green Tin Can arrived. Marlene was already in our usual room, and Wangemann was standing with his hands on her shoulders.

On seeing me, he picked up his club and tapped it lightly against his leg. Suddenly he rushed forward. "Who is behind this conspiracy? Who put you and Guddat up to this?"

"No one."

The club landed across the back of my legs.

"You are lying!" he yelled. "Records show you are connected with a British organization, code name Lord Lister. Who is your British contact? How much are you being paid?"

"Lord Lister was a kids' game. That's all. I've never even met an Englishman."

Wangemann threw his club across the room. It ricocheted off the wall, nearly hitting Müssener. Then he whirled on me, his fist connecting with my jaw. I fell back, my head bouncing off the floor.

Müssener was bending over me when my vision cleared. He helped me up carefully, dabbing the blood from my mouth with his own handkerchief. "I don't know how you can take this, Rudi. It would be best if you tell us everything."

I leaned against him as though he were my mother, crying. "Nobody helped us! Nobody!"

"But you belong to an American church," Müssener said. "If there are American spies in your congregation, you must tell us. Perhaps these are men you have trusted because of your faith. But they have betrayed you. Do you understand, Rudi? They have betrayed and abandoned you."

I shook my head.

"Come now, Rudi, give me their names. Don't protect them anymore."

"I would," I cried. "I would. But I'm telling the truth. Helmuth listened to the BBC. He typed the handbills. I distributed a few of them. That's all."

"You and Karl and Gerhard, you mean."

"We never talked about it. Not knowing was safer."

Müssener nodded. "Okay, Rudi. That's enough for now."

An SS guard took me to the Hall of Mirrors. I was wondering how long I could stand at attention—my strength was nearly gone—when I saw Helmuth.

He was being led away as I was coming in. He looked much worse than I did: his eyes were blackened; his hand was wrapped in a bloody bandage.

Our eyes met for a moment, and Helmuth smiled. His smile seemed apologetic.

I waited in the Hall of Mirrors for an hour. My legs were shaking so hard I could barely stand. Then Müssener called me back to the room.

There were chairs around the table, and he invited me to sit. Marlene wasn't there, and Wangemann wasn't wearing his leather gloves or holding a club. Instead, he held some papers that he placed in front of me.

Müssener set a pen beside my hand. "Read this, Rudi. And sign it," he said.

The papers were a typed account of my interrogation. It ended with these words: "I have read this and found it to be a correct statement."

So Marlene actually worked—she wasn't just Wangemann's girl. Though I'd wondered if she could talk, there was obviously nothing wrong with her hearing—or her writing. Her account was accurate, and I knew I would be condemning myself if I signed it. But I would be condemning myself if I didn't.

I picked up the pen.

Chapter Seventeen

After I signed the confession, the guards stopped interrupting my sleep. For the next three nights—my last in Fuhlsbüttel—I lay on my bunk like a dead man.

The third morning, the guards banged into my cell and marched me to the Green Tin Can. When I stepped onto the bus I realized something was different. There were only three other prisoners on board. And I knew them.

"Helmuth," I whispered. Karl and Gerhard were there, too, handcuffed in place. They'd all been beaten.

Though I'd barely made a sound, the guard heard me and rapped my head sharply with his baton. "No talking," he said, and snapped my handcuffs on to the metal railing. The four of us were as far apart from one another as possible.

My joy quickly faded as the bus started forward. I looked at my friends and felt a stab of anger. If they hadn't given me away, maybe I could have held out. Maybe I'd be home now. Instead I was on the way to a concentration camp. Or my execution.

Suddenly I was filled with shame. How could I point a finger? None of us could have held out. For all I knew, I'd been the first to give in.

A few minutes later, the Green Tin Can pulled into Holstenglacis Prison. We were still in Hamburg, not far from Gestapo headquarters.

The guards herded us out of the bus and into the justice building, where we appeared before a judge. He looked over our files and said, "You'll be here until your trial."

My legs went limp with relief. No executions, at least for now.

The judge noticed my reaction and laughed. "Oh, yes, you'll have a public trial. We want to make an example of you. Until then, enjoy your stay."

From there the guards took us through a tunnel into the prison, where we were processed. Our belongings were waiting for us in large envelopes. While we watched, the guards checked our property against a list. Then they ordered us to shove everything back into the envelopes, which were promptly taken away.

Next the guards issued our uniforms: a jacket without a collar or pockets, pants, and a round hat. Everything was made from dark blue feltlike material.

After showering, we were separated and sent to our cells. Though we were all in Holstenglacis Prison, we were never together while we waited for our indictment papers to arrive.

My cell was so quiet that it nearly drove me crazy. I was alone in a room with a bed, a tiny table, and a stool. During the day, guards spied on me through the peephole to make sure I wasn't lying down. It was against the rules to do anything but stand up or sit on the stool. There was absolutely nothing to do, nothing to read. When I was issued squares of newspaper to use as toilet paper, I would read them when the guards weren't looking.

These guards didn't hit prisoners often—only if you were a troublemaker. The real punishment in Holstenglacis was loneliness and boredom. It was even against the rules to look out the tiny window. Once in a while I grew so hungry for the sky that I'd risk standing on my stool for a glimpse.

The silence worked on your nerves, too. It was a relief each day to have a few minutes of exercise. It was nothing more than running in a single-file line around the courtyard, but at least there was something to hear—guards yelling, shoes rapping against pavement, the chorus of men's heavy breathing.

My days were silent, except for one terrible hour of noise. Nearly every morning between four and five A.M., the guards would take the condemned men to the execution chamber. I could actually hear the giant blade of the guillotine striking home. In some ways, it was even worse to hear the prisoners screaming and shouting, even begging, when the guards would come to take them.

Just when I thought I might go crazy, two things happened that improved my miserable life. First, I was allowed one visitor a month. And second, I was joined by a cellmate. Or rather, I joined him. The guards moved me to another cell, one with two beds and two stools. Things would have seemed perfect, except I could still hear the guillotine.

My new companion was Bernhard Rubinke, who was about eighteen. After days and days of sitting alone with absolutely nothing to do, having someone to talk to was like being in heaven. And we talked about everything—our families, movies, soccer, girls, how much we "loved" the Nazis. Bernhard even wanted to know about my church.

"Why are you here?" I asked Bernhard during our second week together. For some reason, we'd kept quiet about this.

Bernhard glanced toward the peephole. "A little stealing was involved," he said quietly. "But for a good cause."

"Wait, let me guess. The good cause was . . . Bernhard Rubinke," I said.

Bernhard laughed. "It's tough to get by these days," he said, then lowered his voice again. "But at least I went after Hamburg's big-time Nazis. They live a lot better than the rest of us, you know. Things you can't find anywhere else in Hamburg, they've got. Luckily, I was caught stealing food—South American coffee—instead of some of the other things I've made off with, like shortwave radios."

"That was lucky," I said.

"What about you?" Bernhard asked. "I heard you came from Fuhlsbüttel. How was it?"

"It was . . . Who told you?"

"The day before you moved in, I got whacked on the head for staying in the shower too long. Then the guard says to me, 'You don't know how good you got it, Rubinke. Ask your new cellmate. He's just come from Fuhlsbüttel, where they kick the crap out of you for the fun of it.'"

Now I understood why Bernhard hadn't seemed surprised when I was tossed into his cell. Inmates never got any warning about things like transfers, but he'd acted as if he'd been expecting me.

"Is it true? About Fuhlsbüttel?" Bernhard asked. "Are the guards SS?"

"Yes." I touched my face. Most of my bruises

and cuts had healed, but I could feel the scars. "And what the guard told you is true. They hit you with rubber clubs and kick you and laugh the whole time."

"Nobody with a soul would join the SS," Bernhard whispered. "They're all maniacs—especially the Gestapo."

I nodded. "I'm not too popular with the Gestapo right now."

"So what *did* you do, Rudi?"

"Ever listen to one of those shortwaves you picked up?" I asked.

Bernhard smiled. "You broke the radio laws, didn't you?"

I nodded again, then told him about the BBC. And the handbills. And Müssener and Wangemann. And whatever I could remember from the BBC broadcasts.

Bernhard whistled softly. "So Hitler's been lying to us about Russia?"

"He even keeps newspapers from printing soldiers' death notices," I said. "To make us think everything is fine. I hate the Nazis."

Bernhard looked at me with new respect. "Makes my stealing seem like nothing. You're a hero, Rudi. And I'm just a thief."

I shook my head, suddenly nervous. "We shouldn't be talking like this. Someone could hear us."

"Don't worry," Bernhard said. "No one's listening. I thought a spy like you'd have nerves of steel, what with meeting enemy agents in dark alleys and such."

"I'm not a spy," I whispered. Right now Bernhard's joke didn't seem funny. "We should stop now. Okay?"

Bernhard shrugged. "Sure."

From then on, it seemed as if Bernhard always asked questions that could get us in trouble. I'd steer us to other subjects, like Mutti's cooking. But stories about raisin cakes and Wiener schnitzel started to bore him, though my tales of the Lord Lister Detective Agency always made him laugh.

Ten minutes. Not much time for a visitor, but it's all the prison allowed. Mutti came faithfully, but I often wondered if the short visits weren't more like torture for her. She would hold my hand and fight back the tears, and then it would be over. We'd have a whole month to wait for ten more minutes.

191

The routine was always the same. The guards would come for me, and we'd walk through the prison, waiting to pass through steel door after steel door. Then we'd take the tunnel to the justice building, where my mother would be waiting. The trip took much longer than the visit.

We were never alone. A guard and a fellow called a senior government councillor were always in the room. But their presence didn't keep Mutti from complaining about how I was being treated.

The first time she visited, I'd only been in Holstenglacis a week. My bruises and scabs still showed, and when I walked into the room, I thought she was going to faint. She reached for the back of a chair to steady herself and glared at the councillor.

"Rudi, what have they done to you?" she cried.

"Hush, Mutti," I whispered, afraid the guard would report her.

Instead of staying quiet, she turned to the councillor. "What have you done to my boy?"

This could have gone badly for us, but Herr Model was one of the kinder councillors, according to Bernhard. He looked uncomfortable under Mutti's gaze and muttered something about "the Gestapo's work." Then he allowed us an extra five minutes.

On her next visit, Mutti started complaining about my thin face and bony arms. A poor diet—mostly watery soup—had whittled away my bulky frame. "Oh, dear God," she moaned. "My boy is nothing but skin."

Finally, Herr Model gave in and let Mutti bring me a small piece of cake on her other visits. I didn't care a bit that I had to eat it right there in front of him. The glorious sweetness almost made me cry. But when I had cake, I didn't get extra minutes.

Chapter Eighteen

Sometimes I saw Helmuth or Karl or Gerhard during exercise periods, though I never got close enough to talk to them. But our eyes would meet, and we'd nod or wave secretly.

Months went by without a word from the court or the Gestapo. I wondered if they had forgotten about us. Then early in June, my cell door opened, and a man in a dark blue suit stepped inside.

"Rudolf Ollenik?" he asked, looking at Bernhard.

"No, I'm Rudi Ollenik," I said.

He turned to me, clicking his heels. "My name is Beckmann. Please read these papers. I will be back in exactly two hours to retrieve them."

Beckmann pulled a folder from his brief-case. Top Secret was stamped across the front, and a chill settled over me as I reached for it. After he was gone, I sat staring at the papers, not daring to read them.

"You're just a kid, Rudi," Bernhard said, breaking the tense silence. "It won't be that serious—probably Juvenile Court."

I looked up at him, then broke the seal and turned to the first page. The folder contained the indictments for all four of us. It was no surprise that we were charged with "deliberately listening to foreign radio broadcasts" and "willfully distributing newscasts of foreign radio stations." But we were also accused of "lending support to the enemy power"—a charge of "conspiracy to commit high treason."

"What's it say?" Bernhard asked.

"High treason," I whispered.

Bernhard craned his neck to see the papers, and I let him read the charges.

"This may mean Special Court," he said.

I felt hollow inside. The Nazis had set up the Special Courts to take care of disloyal citizens. They passed out concentration camp and death sentences like traffic tickets.

I leafed frantically through the papers, searching for the court assignment. I skimmed past summaries of every handbill and listings of our individual criminal offenses. Then there it was, on the last page.

"So are you headed for Special Court?" Bernhard asked.

I shook my head, fighting the lump in my throat. "We're going to Berlin."

Bernhard stared at me.

"The People's Court!" I cried.

He grabbed the papers, his eyes roving the page. Then he dropped the folder on the table. "What's going on? Why would they send you to the highest court? Unless . . . What haven't you told me, Rudi? Are you working for the Americans? Through your church, maybe?"

"No!"

"If Hitler's blood court is after you, it's for more than tossing around a few handbills." Bernhard glanced at the peephole in our door. "A real American spy! Come on, Rudi. You can tell me."

"Leave me alone," I said, pulling my stool into a corner.

"Don't be mad—I never met anybody important enough for the People's Court, that's all."

Bernhard was acting as if we were talking about a soccer match instead of my life. "Leave me alone," I said. "I need to read this."

Bernhard shrugged. "Whatever you say."

I sat in the corner, facing the wall, but I couldn't concentrate on reading. The People's Court made Special Court look like a Sunday School class. It specialized in spilling German blood.

I calmed down enough to read the indictment papers, searching in vain for a line that would say, "Because Rudolf Ollenik is only sixteen, the court will be lenient." But of course, it wasn't there. Each time I finished, I'd start again, hoping the words would change.

Bernhard shifted uncomfortably, watching me but keeping to himself. Finally, Beckmann returned. As he left with the papers, Bernhard stood and came to my side, dropping a hand on my shoulder. "Sorry," he said, then went back to his stool.

That night I was jerked from sleep again and again by the same dream. The cell door would clang open, and a guard would yell, "Make ready! Your time has come!"

Our trial date was August 11, 1942. That meant sitting in Holstenglacis Prison for two more months. Though I had nightmares about facing the People's Court, it would have been easier to go to Berlin right away. Better to get it over with than stew in my fear for weeks. But at least I got to see Mutti one more time before we left. Herr Model let me eat cake *and* gave us five more minutes. Five more minutes for Mutti to hold my hand and cry.

The day after Beckmann's visit, Bernhard tried to wheedle more from me about my career as a spy, but I'd cut him off. Then the next morning, the guards loaded me into the Green Tin Can and delivered me to Gestapo headquarters.

I was taken straight to a room where Müssener was waiting. Marlene was there, too, but not Wangemann, for which I said a silent prayer of thanks.

"Rudi, I hear you hate all members of the Nazi Party," Officer Müssener said. "I have to tell you, I'm a bit hurt."

His comment took me by surprise. I stood there sputtering, and Müssener laughed.

"Sit down, Rudi," he said. "So you and your friends are going to Berlin. I must say I was a little surprised by that."

There was something different about Müssener. His whole body had been tense and stiff before, but now he slumped comfortably in his chair. Looking at him, I felt the tightness in my own body loosen. Still, I didn't answer.

"Who is your American contact?" he asked.

His voice was sharper, and my eyes flew to his face. But Müssener leaned back, smiling.

His smile gave me confidence, and I answered boldly. "I already told you, no one in my church is a spy. Why are you asking me again?"

"Because you talk too much. You trust people too easily. Poor Rudi."

"Talk too much?" Finally I understood. A chill went through me. "What did Bernhard tell you?"

"That you're mixed up with American spies, for one thing."

"So he's Gestapo," I said dully. "You planted him in my cell."

"You actually think he could be one of us?" Müssener looked insulted. "Again, I'm hurt. Rubinke's been in trouble with the police since he could tie his own shoes. He's been in and out of jail since he was twelve. This time he's in prison for burglary. He hopes we'll lighten his sentence if he finds out something important about you."

"He's lying," I said.

"I don't doubt it."

"Will he be a witness at the trial?"

Müssener waved away my question. "Did Guddat's grandparents listen to the shortwave radio with you?"

"I never said anything about the Sudrows. Never! And I didn't listen to the BBC."

Müssener nodded as if he believed me.

"How can you listen to anything Rubinke tells you?" I cried, silently vowing to get even with Bernhard. "He'd say anything to get out of jail sooner."

"That's enough, Rudi." Müssener sat up in his chair, no longer smiling. "We have to investigate any lead we get, even from the likes of Rubinke. Now answer my questions. Did Mr. and Mrs. Sudrow listen to the BBC?"

"No."

"Did you say that you hate all members of the Nazi Party?"

"No."

"Who is your American contact?"

"No one. I haven't seen an American for three years. Since the Führer threw our missionaries out of Germany."

"Did you and the others commit burglary to finance your operation?"

I almost came out of my chair. "I've never stolen anything in my whole life," I answered. "Not one thing."

Müssener stared at me for several seconds, examining my face closely. "Did you show your indictment papers to Rubinke?"

"Yes."

"They were marked Top Secret and were for your eyes only."

"I didn't think about that. I'm sorry."

"He read the whole document?"

"No. He only saw the page with the charges. And the last page."

Müssener rose from his chair and called for the guards.

"That's all?" I asked.

"Yes," he answered. "But I'll see you in Berlin, Rudi."

As the guards hurried me out to the Green Tin Can, I realized Bernhard had made the mistake of stretching the truth too much. Müssener hadn't taken him seriously. Still, the Gestapo could use his testimony against us. I cursed myself for being so stupid, so trusting, so naive.

My mind was on Bernhard all the way to Holstenglacis. But when the guards pushed me into our cell, he was gone.

I didn't get another cellmate, but I didn't mind. It was safer that way. Yet I kept my eyes open for Rubinke whenever I was out of my cell for exercise periods. Of course, I had no idea how I'd get at Bernhard if I saw him. I figured the guards would keep us apart. That's why I was so surprised when my chance came just a week later.

I almost didn't spot him because Helmuth and Karl were in the same group. I kept trying to sneak a look at them and didn't notice Bernhard was ahead of me only a few places. I happened to see him right before a fight started.

Fights were rare because we were so closely

controlled. In fact, there hadn't been one since I'd been a prisoner. Suddenly, two inmates were rolling on the ground. The guards shouted and swarmed down on them. For a few moments, the rest of us milled about, trying to get a good look at what was happening.

Bernhard still hadn't seen me. He stood, eyes riveted on the flailing men. Now the guards were beating the two, trying to separate them. I edged toward Bernhard, and he noticed me at the last second. His eyes swelled with surprise, but it was too late. My elbow was already headed for his nose.

I moved away quickly while Bernhard fell to his knees, blood gushing from between his fingers. No one noticed, or so I thought. But Helmuth and Karl had used the moment of confusion to try to reach me. They came from opposite directions and were within a few steps when the guards started yelling again. Swiping with their clubs, they forced us back into our lines.

The two fighters lay bloody and unconscious on the ground. As we stood at attention, waiting for them to be hauled away, Karl grinned, flashing me a thumbs-up and nodding toward Bernhard, who was being led to the infirmary. I wondered if he knew Bernhard, too. But Karl would never have trusted a person like him.

Somehow, I escaped punishment for attacking Bernhard. I never knew why. Maybe Bernhard kept his mouth shut. Or maybe the guards thought he got what he deserved. Or maybe they did nothing because they saw nothing. Whatever the reason, the guards never bothered me about it.

I thought I'd feel smug about fixing Rubinke. And smart to get away with it. But I didn't experience the rush of sweet revenge I'd dreamed about. Instead, I felt like Wangemann.

Part Four

Berlin,

1942

Chapter Nineteen

The first week of August, I joined Helmuth, Karl, and Gerhard in the Green Tin Can. We were on our way to Berlin, each of us handcuffed to his own personal guard. At least we were wearing our regular clothes, though they hung loosely on us.

The guards paraded us through the railway station, then led us into a compartment on the train. The windows were covered completely with paper that was stenciled with large letters reading POLICE TRANSPORT—ENTRY FORBIDDEN. As the doors closed and we were sealed off from the outside world, the guards removed our handcuffs.

"Sit over there," Helmuth's guard said,

pointing to the seats along one side of the compartment.

We hurried to sit down before he changed his mind, hardly believing our good fortune. We were together, and unhandcuffed. Even though our guards were Hamburg police rather than SS, I never dreamed they'd let us sit together.

"You may speak to one another," the man said, "but do not stand up. And do not talk about your case."

The guards removed their hats and unbuttoned their gray tunics. They sat in the seats across from ours, talking among themselves. Without getting up, we leaned toward one another, grasping and shaking hands. When Helmuth touched me, hot tears filled my eyes. I threw my arms around him.

None of us could find any words at first. We simply sat there, holding on to one another as if our lives depended on it.

The train was rolling out of Hamburg when Karl finally broke the silence, sitting back with a grin. "What's happened to our mild-mannered Rudi? Clubbing poor Bernhard in the face like that? Prison life has turned you into an animal!"

"You broke his nose," said Helmuth.

"Are you serious?" Gerhard asked. "Rudi broke someone's nose?"

Helmuth nodded. "Rudi's a regular Max Schmeling."

"More like Joe Louis," said Karl. "He's got quick hands like Joe. Or quick elbows, I should say."

"Those fellows are heavyweight boxers," I said. "Look at me. After prison food, I'm more like a paperweight."

Helmuth laughed, then he asked Karl, "You knew that guy?"

"He's a stool pigeon. He was put in Rudi's cell to spy on him."

"How do you know?" I asked.

"Because he was in my cell, too. He would ask such obvious questions! But I didn't know he had been with you until Müssener let it slip."

"Bernhard will probably be a witness," I said, unable to look at Helmuth. "I was stupid enough to trust him."

For one instant, Karl looked surprised. Disappointed. Then he said, "Forget about it, Rudi. He's a snake. Nobody'll believe him.

He's got a police record longer than this train. He's a born liar, and the Gestapo know it."

Gerhard shifted nervously. "Still, I wonder what he told them."

"That we're burglars," I said. "And American spies."

Karl snorted. "What an idiot."

"Helmuth, he told Müssener your grandparents listened to the BBC," I said, tears filling my eyes again. "But I didn't tell him that. I promise, I never said—"

"Stop it, Rudi." Helmuth grabbed my arm. "Bernhard told them what they wanted to hear. You don't have to defend yourself."

"But what if—"

"It's too late for what-ifs, so quit worrying. Besides, if the Gestapo wanted my grandparents, they'd have them by now, and they don't. My grandmother visited me yesterday."

The tears still came as relief washed over me.

"It's all right, Rudi," said Helmuth. "If they use him as a witness, they'll tell him what to say anyway."

"That's enough!" my guard said sharply. "Talk about something else. Last warning."

Helmuth smiled. "Seen any good movies lately?" he asked.

"Yes, I have," said Karl. "The Holstenglacis cinema has been showing some great American pictures."

The guards laughed and stood up to take down the paper so we could see the passing countryside. Then they took out a deck of cards and started a game. For the next four hours they paid little attention to us.

For a while, we all gazed out the window, saying nothing and drinking in the sights. After months of sitting on a stool and staring at the walls, this was better than a trip to the movies. It was as if I'd never seen a tree or a fence or a cow before—or would never see one again.

We rumbled over a bridge, and the spell was broken. Helmuth pulled his eyes from the window and asked, "Remember playing Kippel-Kappel?"

Kippel-Kappel was our favorite game when we were nine or ten. I hadn't thought of it in ages. Karl had always been the best at flipping the Kappel, a stick about twenty centimeters long, so high in the air and so far away that the rest of us would have trouble catching it.

"We'd play until we were dripping with sweat," Karl remembered. "Then we'd go swimming. At the pool or the bathing beaches at the municipal park."

"Trucks would bring in sand for those beaches. I'd nearly forgotten about that," said Helmuth.

"If we didn't swim, we'd go to Stein's bakery," I said. "For bags of cake trimmings. A whole bag for five pfennig."

"And when we didn't have money, we'd go inside just to fill up on the smells." Helmuth sniffed the air. "When I was little, I dreamed of growing up to be Stein's apprentice."

Karl smiled. "Remember when Rudi ate his cake trimmings so fast he got sick?"

Helmuth nodded. "And threw up in the street car . . ."

That's how Helmuth got us started talking about better times. Gerhard joined in, adding his memories to ours, and we kept it up until we reached Berlin. Those were the most pleasant, most peaceful moments I'd had since the day Helmuth showed us the Rola.

Our train shuddered to a stop.

"Fun's over," said Helmuth's guard. "Stand up."

"Thank you," said Helmuth. "For letting us talk."

The guard looked at him in surprise, then nodded curtly.

We stood and were handcuffed. The guards led us from the train car, and, once again, we had to endure whispering and finger-pointing as we shuffled through the station. Outside, a rickety bus waited to take us to Alt-Moabit Prison.

Alt-Moabit made Holstenglacis seem like a fine hotel. First of all, we were welcomed by guards like Tall Paul, only they made certain we weren't hurt where it might show. We needed to look good for the People's Court.

Second, and worst of all, was the filth. I was nearly eaten alive by bedbugs the first night. Soon lice were hopping through my hair and my eyebrows.

Alt-Moabit was old and damp and smelly. Instead of toilets in the cells, we had buckets. The prison stank. Even though we dumped the buckets every morning and rinsed them out, the smell of human waste was always in the air. It mingled with the awful odors of my food, which was slipped through a slot in the cell door. At first it was hard to eat, but when you're hungry enough, you can get used to nearly anything.

And I was hungry enough to eat all they gave me. The slot would open, and the guard would yell, "Eat your swill, pig." I'd plug my nose, swallow whatever was in the bowl, and chew on the hard piece of bread. But after six months of Nazi prison food my weight had dropped by a third.

I was alone in my cell, except for my friends the lice and bedbugs, but I did see Helmuth and the others once or twice a day, either at work detail or during exercise period. Work detail usually meant stuffing mothballs into paper bags, which were set outside the cell doors each night. This only made the smell worse.

Exercise period was a living hell. The guards expected us to do calisthenics, and I was so weak I couldn't keep up. Almost no one could. And if I somehow managed to get through the exercises without being kicked and cursed at, then I was too shaky to climb the stairs back to my cell. So I'd get the swearing and the kicking anyway.

"Traitor!" they'd yell at me. "You're going to be shot or hanged, so maybe we should kill you right now!" But they were bluffing. The People's Court came first.

After four days in Alt-Moabit, the guards came for me. They made sure I was showered and had a clean prison uniform. Then they took me to a room away from the stench and left me to wait alone. Were the Gestapo going to question me again? I imagined Wangemann coming through the door and began to shiver, even though the room was uncomfortably warm.

After about fifteen minutes, the door opened and a man walked in. He wore an expensive suit with a Nazi Party pin on the lapel, but he wasn't Gestapo.

"I'm Dr. Karl Krause, from the National Socialistic Justice Association," he said. "I'm to represent you on August 11."

That I'd have a lawyer never crossed my mind, and here, a few days before the trial, the

215

Nazis sent me one. That meant the others would have attorneys, too. For a moment, I let myself believe that this would make a difference.

Dr. Krause didn't shake my hand. He sat down across the table from me and pulled my indictment papers from his briefcase.

"How are you doing?" he asked. "Holding up, are you?" His voice was friendly enough, but he never once let his eyes meet mine.

"I'm having a great time," I answered coldly. "This is the vacation of my dreams."

"So I see," he said, glancing about the room. "Tell me, what exactly did you do to land yourself in a place like this?"

I stared at Dr. Krause in disbelief. "You're my lawyer, and you don't know?"

"Oh, I know what's in here." He waved the indictment papers. "But I need to hear it from you. Of course, everything you tell me will be held in strictest confidence. The more I know, the better I can help you."

His party pin caught the light, flashing like a warning beacon.

"I passed out a few handbills," I answered. "That's all I did."

"That's all? What about listening to the BBC?"

I shook my head.

"Rudolf, you have to trust me."

"I trust you," I lied. "And I'm telling you the truth. No BBC. No British or American contacts. No stealing to pay for handbills. So you can just forget anything Bernhard Rubinke told you."

Dr. Krause looked surprised, but he recovered quickly. "I have a copy of his report. He's not a credible witness. He won't be called to testify. Now, Rudolf, start at the beginning and tell me everything that happened."

I took a deep breath and did what he asked. But I merely repeated what I'd told Müssener and Wangemann. I'd gone over my "confession" a thousand times, lying alone in my cell, so it was easy to stick to my story. Dr. Krause didn't take any notes.

"What's going to happen to us?" I asked when I was done.

Dr. Krause shrugged. "I think it will turn out for the best. You are only sixteen. That will be my major point of defense."

He slid the indictment papers into his case and stood. "I'll see you at the trial," he said.

After a quick Nazi salute, he was gone. I didn't see him again until the morning I stepped into the courtroom.

Chapter Twenty

I couldn't sleep the night before the trial. Then early in the morning on August 11, the guards came to take me to the showers. Helmuth, Karl, and Gerhard were showering, too. The guards saw to it that we deloused ourselves as best as we could.

Civilian clothes were waiting for us once we were cleaned up. I was surprised to see my suit and white shirt, even a tie. The Gestapo had picked up our Sunday clothes from our parents. The court wanted us to look respectable, as well as louse-free.

"Is that really your suit?" Gerhard asked me.

We were all so thin now that we looked like little boys trying on our fathers' clothes. Two of me could have fit into my pants, so I was fortunate to have suspenders to hold them up. Karl had to use the last hole in his belt, and his trousers were still in danger of slipping to the floor.

When we were dressed, the guards handcuffed us together and loaded us onto the bus. Before eight A.M., we turned onto Bellevuestrasse and arrived at the Berlin Law Courts. The guards took us into the basement and left us in a holding cell until the trial began.

The instant we were alone, Helmuth pulled us close together. "I don't know how much the Gestapo forced out of you," he said, "but I have an idea from the indictment papers." He smiled wryly. "I'll bet we all said more than we wanted to. It's hard not to talk when they're breaking your fingers."

My mind went back to that day in the Hall of Mirrors when I'd seen Helmuth. He'd been bruised and bloody—and his hand had been bandaged. I stared at his fingers and noticed for the first time how crooked and gnarled his left hand was.

Karl's eyes were fastened on Helmuth's

hand, too. "Wangemann?" he asked, his voice hollow.

"Who else?" said Helmuth.

I tried to keep the picture from my mind, but I couldn't. I watched Wangemann twisting Helmuth's fingers until they snapped, and my stomach lurched.

"I want you to know exactly what I told them," Helmuth continued. "Only that you delivered a few handbills. I said that I listened to the Rola by myself. According to the charges, none of you admitted to anything more than passing out handbills. Is that true?"

"Yes," I said. "For me, anyway."

"Same here," said Karl. "But I'm going to tell the judges about listening to the BBC. I won't let you take—"

"Yes, you will," Helmuth said fiercely.

"But—"

"Listen to me! All of you." He leaned in, bringing us even closer. "You will stick to your stories, understand? That's an order!"

"This isn't the army, Helmuth," said Karl. "I don't take orders."

"If you open this door, the Gestapo could go

after everyone we know. Our parents, our friends, the church. You've got to protect them by letting the Nazis believe I'm the only real troublemaker. So keep your mouth shut!"

Karl stared at Helmuth, then dropped his eyes. He nodded.

"How about you, Gerhard?" Helmuth asked.

Gerhard blinked. "Oh . . . right. Just delivering handbills. Except what happened with Herr Mohns. It was no use denying that."

"Mohns? Isn't he the one who turned you in?" I asked.

"That's right," said Helmuth. "Who told you?"

"Your grandmother. She heard what Müssener and Wangemann said when they searched your room."

Gerhard laughed bitterly. "Did she tell you he takes naps in storage rooms?"

Karl looked puzzled.

"That's where we met with Werner," Gerhard said. "Inside a storage room—a safe place, if Mohns hadn't been dozing behind some boxes."

Karl took a deep, shuddering breath. "I thought you'd been really careless, Helmuth.

It's been eating at me all these months. I'm sorry."

"It's not important now," said Helmuth.

"Yes, it is—"

"Be quiet, Karl. We don't have much time, and I want to hear each of you promise me that you'll stick to your stories, no matter what happens. No matter what they do to me."

We looked at the floor, none of us answering.

"Promise!" he cried, thrusting out his hand.

I nodded slowly and reached out to cover his hand with mine. Karl and Gerhard did the same.

"Good," said Helmuth. "I know this is how God wants it."

A terrible feeling of doom settled over us after making our pledge to Helmuth. We sat or stood or paced back and forth, barely speaking, until our attorneys arrived and led us into the courtroom.

"Look at this place," Karl whispered.

Three bloodred swastika banners hung from the high ceilings. Marble busts of Frederick the Great and Adolf Hitler decorated the room, staring coldly down on us. And on the wall above the judges' bench hung a giant golden eagle perched on a swastika. The prisoners in Alt-Moabit had called it the vulture of destruction.

Spectators—mostly newspaper reporters—were already sitting in the gallery. I tried not to look at them as we filed in, but I saw Karl raise his hand and wave just before we sat down.

"My father is here," he said huskily.

I turned to look for my mother and was relieved when I couldn't find her. I don't know how Karl felt, but I didn't want my family to see this. As it turned out, his father was the only one of our relatives allowed to attend.

As my eyes swept across the room, I felt more hopeless than ever. The chamber itself made you feel small and vulnerable. Platforms of different heights rose from the front—the more important you were, the higher you sat. We were placed far below and to the left of the judges' bench, sitting behind our lawyers.

Suddenly, doors swung open and the crowd hushed.

"Stand," a man commanded.

Seven men marched into the courtroom, three of them in bloodred caps and robes. The other men were in dressed in SS, Wehrmacht, or Nazi Party uniforms.

Dr. Krause leaned back and whispered, "The first two—the ones in the robes—are full-time justices of the People's Court. Justice Engert is the vice president of the court, but Justice Fikeis will be presiding today. The other man in a robe is Attorney General Drullman."

"And the others?" I asked.

"Invited by the court to serve as judges. You can tell by their uniforms what government or military groups they represent."

Justice Fikeis cleared his throat. "Heil Hitler!" A chorus of "Heil Hitlers" filled the courtroom. "In the name of the German people, I call this court to order. Justice Engert will read the charges against the accused."

"Stand when I call your name," Justice Engert said. "And acknowledge if I have stated it correctly. Helmuth Hübener."

Helmuth exploded from his chair. "My name is Guddat, Helmuth *Guddat.*"

"It was Guddat," Engert said. "Your step-father—a loyal Party member—has legally adopted you. Not that you deserve such an honor."

Karl and I looked at each other in surprise.

"I'm Guddat," Helmuth said.

225

Engert's eyes bored into him. "Helmuth Hübener, what is your birth date?"

"January 8, 1925," he answered, his voice defiant.

"Residence?"

"Alt-Moabit Prison."

Soft laughter rippled through the gallery. Helmuth's attorney stood and whispered in his ear.

Helmuth sighed and answered again. "Hamburg. Louisenweg 137."

"That is not your address!" Engert yelled. "You'd better keep your client in line, Dr. Knie."

Helmuth looked confused for a moment, then he raised his eyes to the ceiling. "Sachsenstrasse 42," he said. "But that's Hugo Hübener's address. I've never lived there."

"Occupation?" asked Engert.

"Administrative apprentice, Hamburg Social Services," Helmuth answered, his voice dull now.

Justice Engert then read the charges against him. They were more serious than mine. They named Helmuth as the ringleader who listened to foreign broadcasts, produced flyers and full-page handbills, and then lured the rest of us into his web.

When Engert was finished with Helmuth, we each had our turn. Next, he asked our attorneys if they had anything to say. "No," they answered. Four lawyers, and not one said anything in our defense.

Then Justice Fikeis took over. "Hübener, give the Führer's birth date," he barked. Then he followed with more stupid questions. "Ollenik, how many points in the Nazi Party Program?" "Schneider, what are the words of the 'Horst Wessel Song'?" It was more like a Gestapo interrogation than a trial.

We were so worn out it was hard to think. Even simple questions were difficult. Only Helmuth stood up under the attack—it was as if the weeks of torture and starvation hadn't bothered him at all. His answers were sharp and defiant, and he always answered in great detail, whether the question required it or not. When Fikeis asked Hitler's birth date, Helmuth added the Führer's birthplace, parents' names, mother's maiden name, schooling, rank in the army during World War I, and kept adding until the judge yelled at him to be quiet.

"As you can see," Justice Fikeis said when the quiz was over, "our young Herr Hübener is the brilliant one of this shoddy little group. You all heard his bold answers. The boy is a deep and dangerous thinker. Don't let his youthful appearance fool you."

He lifted a folder from the desktop. "I have here further evidence that we are not dealing with the mind of a child. This is a political essay, titled 'The War of the Plutocrats.' It was written by Hübener as part of his final school examination, for which he received top honors. A few of the judges of this tribunal have read the paper, and now I would like for the court to hear their responses."

Attorney General Drullman leaned forward to speak. "When I first saw this essay, I would not believe a fifteen-year-old boy had written it. So we confirmed the fact with Hübener's teachers. They assured us this was his work." He shook his head in amazement. "A first-year student in law school would receive the highest marks for this paper."

The gallery buzzed at Drullman's statement, and Fikeis had to quiet them.

"It is plain that Hübener is an adult—at least, intellectually," said Justice Engert. "He may be morally stunted, but mentally, he is every bit an adult. Therefore, it is clear that he should not be tried as a juvenile."

The other judges nodded in agreement.

Fikeis ordered us to stand. "I've been waiting for weeks to see you in person," he said. "To see the brazen children who dared to slander our Führer. You are beyond belief. Decent Germans—decent human beings—could never speak against the hero who freed us from our enemies. Who returned the Fatherland to its greatness. Who is our savior. So you boys are not decent human beings. You are not human at all. And for your blasphemy, each of you deserves to die."

The courtroom was deathly silent. Everyone knew that the judges were also the jury, so Fikeis's words hung heavy in the air.

Chapter Twenty-one

Only four men testified, every one of them a witness for the Gestapo. Our lawyers didn't ask a single question. The first witness was young and wore an army uniform. When he entered the courtroom, Gerhard stirred nervously.

"State your name, birth date, occupation, and residence," said Fikeis.

"Horst Zumsande. February 9, 1924. I've recently joined the Wehrmacht, as you see. I'm stationed in Thorn now, but before that I lived in Hamburg, Grindelalle 6."

"Make your statement."

Horst shifted uncomfortably. "My brother and I have known Gerhard Bauer for several years. One night in January he visited us at our apartment. We were planning to play cards, but Gerhard pulled out a handbill and asked us to read it. It was enemy propaganda, so we gave it back to him.

"I threatened to report him, but he laughed and said I'd have no proof. When he left I made notes of anything I could remember from the paper he'd shown us. I planned to turn him in if I got more evidence, but he never talked about such things again."

Next, Fikeis called Werner Kranz. I'd been waiting to see him finally.

"Make your statement," Fikeis said.

"I work in the same office as Helmuth Gud—Hübener and Gerhard Bauer. On January 17, 1942, they came to me, asking about my French." Werner paused, smiling. "I'm very good, I told them. Of course, Gerhard knew this already, from our days together in school. Then they asked me to do them a favor. They needed some things translated."

Helmuth was staring intensely at Werner, who was careful to look away from us.

"'Sure,' I told them. 'If it won't take too long.' When I asked what they wanted translated, Helmuth said, 'It's a secret. Can you keep a secret?' I laughed and said that I could. That was before I knew what they were up to."

"And what were they 'up to'?" Fikeis asked.

"A few days later they pulled me into a storage room at work and showed me one of their handbills, which they asked me to translate. They wanted to distribute them to French prisoners. I told them to leave me out of it. Herr Mohns overheard us. Later, I told him everything. That's the last I had to do with this."

Fikeis dismissed Werner and called for Heinrich Mohns. A puffy little man strutted into the courtroom. I realized with a shock that I'd never seen any of these witnesses before today—and they held my life in their hands.

"I'd had my eye on Hübener for some time," Mohns said. "No particular reason, just a feeling I had about him. So I hid myself in the storage room where he sometimes met with his friends. That's when I overheard his conversation with Kranz."

"Did you confront Hübener and Bauer right away?" asked Fikeis.

"No." Mohns tapped a finger against his forehead. "I decided to lay a trap. Later I found

Kranz and asked him to try to get some handbills from Hübener. He agreed to help but told me that I'd probably have a better chance with Bauer."

"You could get the handbills from Gerhard Bauer?"

Mohns said, "Bauer had told Kranz that he was having second thoughts. So I confronted Bauer the next day, and he gave me two handbills. Of course, I contacted the Gestapo immediately."

"Of course," said Fikeis.

Karl glared at Gerhard, but Helmuth didn't change his expression, just sat there calmly. I felt like I'd been punched in the stomach.

Then Müssener took Mohns's place on the stand. He gave a quick overview of our confessions, starting with Helmuth's. It was clear that he saw Helmuth as the ringleader, the real threat.

When it was my turn, Müssener surprised me by bringing up Bernhard.

"Rudolf Ollenik's former cellmate reported that Ollenik admitted listening to the BBC," he said. "This informer, Bernhard Rubinke, is not entirely trustworthy—however, I believe this part of his story because I always felt Ollenik was lying to me about the BBC."

Müssener could have used more of Bernhard's report against me, so I was relieved when he moved on to Gerhard. In the middle of reviewing Gerhard's statement, he paused.

"Bauer denies serious involvement with Hübener," he said. "In fact, Bauer's statement includes this sentence: 'It was my goal to gather handbills and keep them safe until the proper time came to expose Guddat'—meaning Hübener, of course."

Karl started, and I thought he might actually try to get at Gerhard. But Helmuth placed his hand on Karl's arm, and he quieted.

Müssener continued, "I'm not convinced this is true. Bauer certainly had enough material to come forth long before he was arrested, yet he did not. Until Herr Mohns confronted him."

"Is there anything else, Officer?" Fikeis asked.

"One other thing," said Müssener. "The three Mormon boys—Hübener, Schneider, and Ollenik—have shown affinity for things British since they were young schoolchildren. Four or five years ago, they created a game called the Lord Lister Detective Agency, named after a series of British mystery novels. At first we wondered if—once they were older—they had sought out British contacts. But we were unable to find any connections of this sort. However, they do belong to an American church. These strong ties to the English-speaking world may have led to their otherwise unexplainable behavior."

When Müssener finished, Justice Fikeis called a lunch recess. We were herded out of the courtroom and back to the holding cell.

The moment the guards were gone, Karl erupted. He leaped forward, pushing me aside, and swung at Gerhard, knocking him to the floor.

Karl stood over him, his fists still clenched. "You were setting us up all along!"

Helmuth stepped between them. Karl tried to push him, but Helmuth stood firm. "Stop it," he said. "Müssener was right. This time we can trust the Gestapo. If Gerhard had planned to turn us in, he would have done it sooner."

"What about giving Mohns the handbills?" Karl asked, his voice shaking with anger.

"I didn't," Gerhard said quietly. "He had me searched, and I was stupid enough to have them on me, in case Werner changed his mind. Mohns lied about that. I never had second thoughts."

"Mohns lied about everything," Helmuth said to Karl. "We'd never been in that storage room before. And his talk about keeping his eye on me—Mohns was too busy ducking work to watch anyone."

"But Gerhard told Müssener he'd planned all along to turn us in," I said.

Gerhard's eyes filled with tears. "I said it because I was scared. And the pain . . . I'm sorry. I'm so sorry." He turned his head away, and his body shook as he wept.

Forty-five minutes passed in silence. We were spread about the room, each of us lost in his private thoughts. Then the cell door rattled and swung open, and Hugo Hübener stepped into the room.

Helmuth stood and took one step toward him. The rest of us stood, too, and backed away.

"How's Mother?" Helmuth asked.

Hugo stepped briskly forward and took Helmuth's shoulders in his hands. "She's fine. And sends her love to you."

Helmuth nodded, a wistful smile playing about his mouth.

Hugo dropped his hands. "I know you . . . don't care for me," he said. "But I want you to know what I've done to help you. Your mother and I processed the adoption papers because we thought connecting you to the SS might help."

Helmuth stiffened. "My name is Guddat."

"I don't think it made much difference anyway," said Hugo. "But who knows? Maybe your sentence will be lightened."

"The trial isn't over yet," said Helmuth. "Maybe I won't be sentenced at all."

Hugo started to say something but bit back his words.

Helmuth smiled. "I'm joking."

There was a deep sadness in Hugo's eyes. "This isn't a joking matter," he said softly.

"I know," said Helmuth.

They stood staring at each other until a guard's voice interrupted. "It's time. Let's go."

"Well, they didn't give us long," said Hugo. "I doubt they'll let me see you again."

"Give my love to Mother. And to my grandparents," Helmuth said. Then he reached out and took Hugo's hand. "Thanks for trying."

Chapter Twenty-two

The guards marched us back to the courtroom. When we'd taken our places, Justice Fikeis immediately cleared the spectators from the gallery.

"We will be examining sensitive documents," he explained, "that we consider to be a national security risk."

When the spectators were gone, the judges brought out copies of our handbills. One by one, Engert read them aloud. Some of the judges had clearly never seen Helmuth's work before. One of them shouted, "Hübener! Why did you do this?"

Helmuth seemed to rise to twice his height, his voice strong and confident. "I wanted the German people to know the truth."

"The truth!" Fikeis sneered. "What do you know about the truth? Are you stupid enough to believe the British?"

"Are you stupid enough to believe everything the German Armed Forces News tells you?" Helmuth asked in return.

"You will regret your insolence," said Fikeis. "Now answer plainly. Do you believe the British?"

"Yes. And if you listened to the BBC, you would, too."

The judges fell silent.

Then Engert asked, "Do you doubt Germany's superiority? Do you doubt we will win this war?"

Helmuth raised his chin, his eyes sweeping across the line of judges. "We've made nearly the whole world our enemy. How can we possibly win?"

All seven judges erupted, their loud voices mixing in a meaningless jumble of sound. When they finally settled down, Fikeis spoke, his voice low and threatening. "We have seen enough, and we have heard enough. But before we withdraw to deliberate, we will hear from the attorneys for the defense."

None of the attorneys took more than a few seconds, asking only that the judges be lenient because of our age. Dr. Knie added a request that the court order a psychiatric examination for Helmuth. "From his behavior, it seems likely that the boy is not sane," he said. "Perhaps, with treatment, he can be rehabilitated."

Rehabilitated? Insanity was a crime punishable by death in Nazi Germany, so what was Dr. Knie trying to do?

The judges filed from the courtroom while guards allowed the spectators to flow back inside. Karl turned and looked for his father, but I kept my eyes on Helmuth, who sat stiffly in his chair. Why had he done this? Been so bold, so defiant?

I hadn't yet been able to admit to myself what Helmuth already understood and accepted. He was going to die. To make his death stand for something, he had remained true to himself and what he believed.

In twenty minutes, the judges marched back in. When they'd taken their places, a hush settled over the room.

"The defendants will rise," Fikeis called out to us. "You four are no better than Communists or Jews. You are traitors to the Fatherland. You are vermin, and for the Fatherland to survive, the vermin among us must be exterminated." He stared at us with such hatred that I shivered.

Fikeis lifted a document and began to read from it. "The court orders the following to be sentenced. Hübener, for listening to a foreign radio station and distributing the news in connection with conspiracy to commit high treason and treasonable support of the enemy: death."

Helmuth began to sway a little, then grasped the railing and forced himself to stand upright.

"Hübener also will be denied his civil rights for the remainder of his life," Fikeis said. "Ollenik . . ."

Karl reached out and held my arm.

"Ollenik, for listening to a foreign radio station and distributing foreign radio news in connection with conspiracy to commit high treason: ten years imprisonment.

"Schneider, for distributing foreign radio news: five years imprisonment; and Bauer, for distributing foreign radio news: four years imprisonment.

"Ollenik, Schneider, and Bauer will be credited five months for time already served," Fikeis continued. "The Rola radio and Remington typewriter are to remain impounded, and the defendants are to bear the costs of these proceedings. Do you have anything to say? Ollenik?"

I was filled with a terrible remorse that I could feel such relief when Helmuth was going to die. I shook my head in shame.

"Schneider?"

"No," he answered.

"Bauer?"

Gerhard raised his eyes to Fikeis. "I lied," he said. "I was one with Helmuth from the beginning. I—"

Fikeis's laughter cut him off. "You could never be one with Hübener. You lack his courage and his intelligence. It's your turn, Hübener."

Helmuth spoke, his voice firm. "You've sentenced me to die for telling the truth. My time is now, but let me tell you this—your time will come. You will answer to man and to God for your evil. You and Hitler and all the Nazis."

"Get them out of my sight!" Fikeis shouted at the guards.

They hurried forward and handcuffed us, then led us out. We passed through a crowd waiting beyond the doors. Karl's father reached out to touch him. "Be strong," I heard someone whisper.

We were led to a different room, larger than our previous holding cell. The guards brought us some bread and some coffee and uncuffed us—except for Helmuth, whose hands were behind his back.

"What about him?" Karl asked.

The guards laughed.

Karl broke the bread into bite-sized pieces and fed them to Helmuth. "They won't go through with it. They just want to give you a good scare, teach you a lesson. They'll change your sentence."

"Karl's right," I agreed. "You're too young, Helmuth. In a few days they'll give you a sentence more like ours." But I didn't believe what I was saying, and the sound of my voice showed it.

"I don't usually agree with Mormons," said Gerhard, trying to smile. "But I think they're right about this." His voice sounded as empty as mine.

"See there? We all feel the same way," said Karl, lifting the tin coffee cup to Helmuth's lips.

But Helmuth turned away from the cup to stare at the wall. "No," he said quietly, "they'll kill me."

For the first time I noticed the walls were covered with scribblings: "Farewell, my dear Margo." "Good-bye, Mother." "I do not want to die." "Marie, take care of the children." "God, help us all."

There were names and Bible verses and brief notes written or scratched everywhere, even on the iron door. Many were in foreign languages I couldn't understand, but that didn't matter. Their meaning was clear—they were tombstones.

"Their last chance to say good-bye," said Helmuth. "I need a pencil. Something to write with."

"No, Helmuth," Karl said. "Don't think like this."

"It might be my last chance, too. I can't pass it by." Helmuth smiled, and I thought my heart would break. "Please help me," he said.

So we searched the cell—the windowsill, the ledge above the door, every crack and crevice. Then under the table, wedged into a loose joint in the wood, I found the stub of a pencil, still sharp enough to work. I wondered who had hidden it so carefully for us to find.

Next, we searched the walls for a free spot. Karl found the best place, but I kept the pencil, determined to write for Helmuth.

"What do you want to say?" I asked.

Helmuth drew near. "Karl, Rudi—we grew up together. We're like brothers. So I'll leave it to you to say good-bye to my mother and my grandparents. And the people at church."

"But we'll be locked up for years," I said.

"Maybe you'll get visitors. You can send the messages with them. Somehow you can do this for me, even if it means waiting until you're free. Besides, you won't be in prison ten years. The Allies will set you free long before that."

"Stop talking like this!" Karl cried. "You're not dead yet! There's still a chance you'll make it. And what about God? He could save you. We'll fast and pray. The branch members will pray for you, too. You can't give up hope."

"I won't give up hope," Helmuth said. "But

like I've said before, even prophets in the scriptures were killed. So why not me?" He took a
deep breath. "Here's what I want you to write,
Rudi. . . ."

It was a verse from the New Testament—
one we'd used in our scripture chases back in
MIA. Carefully, I wrote the words: *And ye shall
know the truth, and the truth shall make you free—
John 8:32.* Under this I wrote *Helmuth Guddat,
11 August 1942.*

"Thank you, Rudi," Helmuth said. "Now
hide the pencil for the next man."

Karl finished feeding Helmuth the rest of
the bread, and we talked of home and what
we planned to do after the war was over—
anything to lighten the heavy weight pressing
on our souls. Then Karl suggested that we
kneel together and pray, and though this was
strange to Gerhard, he agreed. But as we fell to
our knees, the cell door opened. Our time
together was done.

"Schneider. Ollenik. Bauer. It's back to Alt-
Moabit for you. Hübener stays here—for now."

In turn, we each hugged Helmuth, our tears
mingling. It was the last time I ever saw my
friend.

Chapter Twenty-three

Berlin, 27 October 1942

The Attorney General
of the People's Court
8J 127/42

Present:
First Public Prosecutor Ranke
    as Director of Execution
Clerk of the Justice Department Renk
    as Executive of the Secretariat

The undersigned official of the Reich's Attorney General's Office of the People's Court, today visited the penal institution Plötzensee in Berlin for the purpose of executing the condemned prisoner

Helmuth Hübener

who was legally sentenced to death on 11 August 1942.

The executioner from Berlin, Röttger, reported to the officers that he and his assistants were ready to commence with the execution. In the foreground stood a table covered with a black tablecloth, upon which were placed a crucifix and two burning candles. The back of the room was separated from the rest by a black curtain, which hid the guillotine from view.

The undersigned officers took their place behind the table and the executioner took his place with his three assistants in front of the closed curtain. Also present was First Inspector of Administration, Rohde.

The Director of Executions then ordered the condemned prisoner to be escorted into the room. At 8:13 P.M. the condemned man appeared with his hands shackled behind his back. Two prison guards escorted him into the room, locking the door behind them.

The Director of Executions then identified the condemned man as the one sentenced to death by the People's Court on 11 August 1942 and told the executioner to proceed. Immediately, the curtain was withdrawn and the three executioner's assistants took hold of the condemned man, who was calm. The prisoner showed no resistance when he was placed before the guillotine. With his shirt removed, he was placed upon the apparatus and the executioner removed the head from the body of the condemned man with the guillotine. He then reported the sentence carried out.

The procedure took ten seconds from the time the condemned entered the room until he was turned over to the executioner, and eight seconds from when he was turned over to the executioner until the executioner reported that the sentence had been carried out.

Ranke
Renk

Epilogue

Karl, Gerhard, and I survived the war. We had a close call or two, but God let us live to tell Helmuth's story.

After a few more days in Berlin, the Nazis took us back to Hamburg, then to nearby Glassmoor Prison Camp. While we were in Glassmoor, the news reached us that Helmuth was dead.

Before long, the Allies began bombing Hamburg both day and night. Even as far out as Glassmoor we could feel the earth shake, hear the distant roar, and feel the wind as air rushed in to feed the fires. After the war, I found out that the bombs had killed Brother and Sister Sudrow.

Soon the three of us were sent to a work camp in Poland. I thanked God that we were able to stay together. Then the Russians began to push the Wehrmacht back, and we found ourselves marching toward home in the dead of winter. We nearly froze to death as the guards forced us forward.

We nearly starved, too, but Karl always managed to find us something to eat just when our strength was gone. By God's grace, we made it back to Glassmoor, though Gerhard's frozen feet had crippled him. Then Karl, who had served half of his sentence by that time, was pulled out of camp and made a soldier in Hitler's army.

As it turned out, Helmuth was right about me. I did not serve my ten-year sentence. The war ended in 1945, and the British set Hamburg free. But Karl was captured by the Russians, and I didn't see him again until 1949. By the time he was released, he had been a prisoner for seven years.

And what of Helmuth? We worried that no one would remember his courage, but he became a hero in the new Germany. It didn't even matter that he was now known by his stepfather's name—what mattered was that his death meant something. Helmuth was a symbol of moral courage to a new generation of Germans.

In 1952, Karl moved to America. A year later, I followed. We both settled in Salt Lake City in the state of Utah—the home of our church headquarters. I know Helmuth would have loved to have joined us there.

In some ways, I feel he has.

Author's Note

Brothers in Valor: A Story of Resistance is based on the true story of the Helmuth Hübener Group, German teenagers who resisted Hitler. The novel closely follows the accounts given by Rudolf Wobbe (Rudi Ollenik in this novel) and Karl-Heinz Schnibbe (Karl Schneider), Helmuth's fellow resisters. Some years after World War II, each of them wrote a biography recounting his experience with the Hübener Group. Because I fictionalized their stories and personalities, I changed the last names of all the boys involved in the resistance movement, except for Helmuth. It somehow didn't seem right to alter his name. Helmuth's fourth accomplice, Gerhard Düwer is called Gerhard Bauer here.

The Nazi government kept detailed records, and most of the documents concerning Helmuth Hübener, including his handbills and the report of his execution, came from Nazi archives. Brigham Young University professors Blair R. Holmes and

Alan F. Keele translated these documents—including the ones I used in *Brothers in Valor*—and published them in a book about the Helmuth Hübener Group entitled *When Truth Was Treason*. Readers may find interesting the following bits of additional information about this story.

· The Gestapo's reaction to the LORD LISTER DE-TECTIVE AGENCY may seem unrealistic. However, when the Nazis planned the invasion of Great Britain, the Boy Scouts were on their list of the most dangerous organizations.

· After the four boys were sentenced, many individuals and organizations appealed for leniency. Even the Gestapo and Helmuth's Hitler Jugend Group wrote letters begging for clemency.

· Helmuth was the first juvenile to receive a death sentence for listening to foreign radio broadcasts. His body, like those of many executed by the People's Court, was donated to the Anatomical Institute of the University of Berlin for medical experiments.

· School children not only did math problems about eradicating the mentally disabled and other groups the Nazis thought inferior, but also took field trips to hospitals to be shown that such killings were humane.

· Branch President Arthur Zander made sure that Helmuth was excommunicated from The Church of Jesus Christ of Latter-day Saints. Many members of the church did not support this action. After the war, church officials reinstated Helmuth as a member in good standing.

· There were a few other valiant Germans who resisted Hitler's power, such as Hans and Sophie Scholl. These college students were instrumental in organizing The White Rose and began to distribute leaflets calling for the overthrow of the Nazi government. Hans and Sophie were also sentenced to death by the People's Court and died on February 22, 1943.

Other young Germans who resisted the Nazis include the Edelweiss Pirates and the Swing Youth. The Edelweiss Pirates attacked Hitler Jugend members, distributed anti-Nazi literature, and were even involved in assassinating the Gestapo Chief of the city of Cologne. Twelve young Edelweiss Pirates from Cologne were hanged in 1944.

The Swing Youth were high school students who loved American swing music and jazz, which were considered depraved and treasonous by the Nazis. When they refused to give up their music and dancing, the Gestapo arrested and imprisoned many of them.

· The Church of Jesus Christ of Latter-day Saints had been in Germany since the 1840s but was considered an American church and therefore was under suspicion by the Nazis. Many German Mormons supported Hitler in the beginning, mostly because of a religious principle called The Twelfth Article of Faith: "We believe in being subject to kings, presidents, rulers, and magistrates, in obeying, honoring, and sustaining the law." However, unlike Arthur Zander, not many church members joined the Nazi Party. Eventually it became clear to nearly all Mormons that Hitler stood for the opposite of their Christian beliefs.

I wish to thank Karl-Heinz Schnibbe for his help with this manuscript both through his writings and through the interviews he granted me so graciously. Though Rudi Wobbe died in 1992, his biography (written with Jerry Borrowman) was also invaluable to my project, and I would like to thank him. Thanks also go to Blair Homes and Alan Keele, whose scholarly work (*When Truth Was Treason*) about the Hübener Group contributed many important historical details and provided me with the translated handbills and other documents.

A Selected Timeline
of World War II

–1933–

January 30   Adolf Hitler becomes
                     Germany's Chancellor.

–1936–

October 25   Germany and Italy sign the
                     Italo-German Axis pact.

November 25   Germany and Japan also sign
                     an alliance.

–1938–

March 12   German troops enter Austria.

October 1   German troops occupy the
                     Sudentenland in Czechoslo-
                     vakia.

November 9–10   Kristallnacht

–1939–

September 1   Germany invades Poland.

September 3   Great Britain and France
                     declare war on Germany.
                     World War II begins.

–1940–

May 12	Germany invades France.
June 22	France surrenders.
September 27	Germany, Italy, and Japan form a military pact.

–1941–

May 10	Rudolf Hess flees to England.
June 22	Hitler attacks the Soviet Union.
September 1	All Jews in Germany are ordered to wear yellow stars.
December 7	Japan bombs Pearl Harbor.
December 8	Great Britain and the United States declare war on Japan.
December 11	Germany and Italy declare war on the United States. The United States declares war on Germany and Italy.

–1942–

January 20	At the Wannsee Conference, Hitler determines his "Final Solution" for the "Jewish problem."

–1943–

| February 2 | German troops surrender to the Soviets at Stalingrad. |
| September 9 | Allied troops land in Italy. |

–1944–

June 6	D-Day. Allied troops land in France.
June 23	Soviet summer offensive begins.
December 16	The Battle of the Bulge, the last great German counter-offensive, begins.

–1945–

April 30	Hitler commits suicide.
May 7	Germany surrenders unconditionally. The war in Europe ends.
August 14	Japan surrenders unconditionally. World War II ends.